HER

A NOVEL

NEW YORK TIMES BESTSELLING AUTHOR
Carey Heywood

*Jenifer,
Live, Love, Read!
♡
Carey Heywood*

Her
Copyright © 2013 by Carey Heywood

Cover by Okay Creations
(http://www.okaycreations.com)
Edited by Yesenia Vargas
Interior Designed by Jovana Shirley, Unforeseen Editing
(http://www.unforeseenediting.com)

All rights reserved. Except as permitted under the U.S. Copyright Act of 1976, no part of this publication may be reproduced, distributed, or transmitted in any form or by any means, or stored in a database or retrieval system, without prior written permission of the author.

The scanning, uploading, and distribution of this book via the Internet or via other means without the permission of the publisher is illegal and the punishable by law. Please purchase only authorized electronic editions and do not participate in or encourage electronic piracy of copyrighted materials. Your support of the author's rights is appreciated.

Her is a work of fiction. Names, characters, places, and incidents are either the product of the author's imagination or are used fictitiously. Any resemblance to actual persons, living or dead, events, or locales is entirely coincidental.

ISBN-13: 978-0-9887713-9-0

Other Books

A Bridge of Her Own

Uninvolved

Stages of Grace

Him

*For Zachary,
you gave me the strength to fight for my dreams.*

CONTENTS

Chapter 1 1
Chapter 2 15
Chapter 3 29
Chapter 4 47
Chapter 5 65
Chapter 6 81
Chapter 7 101
Chapter 8 115
Chapter 9 131
Chapter 10 139
Chapter 11 151
Chapter 12 159
Chapter 13 171
Chapter 14 179
Chapter 15 197
Chapter 16 211
Chapter 17 233
Chapter 18 259
Chapter 19 279
Chapter 20 301
Acknowledgments 313
About the Author 315

1

There's this girl. She's in my English class. She sits in the desk next to mine. I see her everyday, but I've never really noticed her.

We've been paired up to do a project on the book *Sarah, Plain and Tall*, which is funny since that's her name too. Yesterday, I went over to her house to work on it. At first, she had asked if we could meet at my house, but I'd rather be anywhere else. Sarah and I went to different schools last year. Kids from my old school already knew I never invited anyone over.

This is the first time I have ever hung out with someone who lives outside of my neighborhood. She gives me directions to her house, and I ride my bike over. Her house is a lot smaller than mine, but I like it. It feels like a family lives there. I can't remember the last time I felt like that in my house.

She's so quiet at first. I keep having to ask her to repeat herself. After a while, I don't have to. We hang out in her kitchen. Her mom is working around us, making dinner. She invites me to stay and eat with them, telling me to call my mom first to make sure it's okay.

I use their cordless, but I only pretend to call. It doesn't matter. My mom won't notice if I'm there or not.

Sarah has an older brother named Brian. He seems cool. I've never really hung out with someone in high school before.

When I go home that night and have to walk past Bethany's room to get to mine, I almost wish I was still at Sarah's.

I'm going back there today to work on our project some more. Maybe her mom will invite to me eat with them again. It'd be nicer than microwaving a hot dog like I do most nights. There's something about her house that makes me feel like I can relax.

Sarah is so nervous and for what? We kill it. Sure getting up in front of the whole class can suck, but I do most of the talking. I glance over at her as we sit back down. She gives me a shy smile. The next pair to go up are Mariah Osborne and Kelly Sotello. They have a shoebox, another diorama. I like Sarah's cereal box idea. It was creative. They're being weird about their project, though. Most people hold their project up first so everyone can see it. The lid is still on theirs.

Mrs. Hall notices too and asks them to take the lid off. When they do, there're a couple of gasps from the front row. Sarah and I sit towards the back so I squint at it, trying to see it better. It looks like the farm from the book, with a couple of people standing in front of it. During each of the oral presentations, the project part gets passed around the room for everyone to get a chance to see. I can hear people snickering and looking back in our direction as it makes its way around the room.

I get it before Sarah. What the fuck? Now I know what everyone is laughing about. Sarah reaches out for it. I shake my head. There is no way I'll let her see this. Mariah and Kelly have taped a picture of Sarah's face over the doll in the diorama. Everyone is watching us now. Kelly looks smug, and Mariah looks nervous. I have a feeling it wasn't her idea.

Sarah just looks at me confused. "Will?"

Mrs. Hall walks over to us. "Is there a problem, Mr. Price?"

Shit. I wait for her to get to my desk and tilt it so Sarah can't see it, only I don't know she has gotten out of her chair and is standing behind me until I hear her gasp. I turn back in time to see her, eyes wide, hand covering her mouth before she runs out the room. I set the diorama on my desk and look at Mrs. Hall. She nods her head, and I get up to run after Sarah. Kelly flinches as I pass her. What a bitch. I pause at the door. I hadn't seen which way she went. Luckily, she hasn't gone far.

She's halfway between our class and the next room over, sitting up against the wall, her head in her hands.

Once I get closer, I can tell she's crying. She's making sniffling noises, and her shoulders are shaking. I didn't really think before I ran after her. I don't know what to do. I just want her to stop crying.

I slowly sit down next to her. "Are you okay?"

She doesn't say anything, just shakes her head.

"Those girls are jerks. Don't pay attention to them." I think about putting my arm around her, but that would be weird so I knock her elbow with mine.

She lifts her head up a little and looks at me. Her eyes seem so big, and I can see them just brimming with tears.

"Why would they do that?" Her voice is so small.

Shit. I didn't really know her before we worked on the project together. She's cool, really cool. "Some people are just assholes."

"I never—" Her voice breaks. "Did anything to them."

I watch one plump tear crest then roll down her cheek. She's right. I don't know her that well, but I can tell the kids who are jerks from the ones who aren't. Sarah's quiet. She hangs back. If we weren't paired up, I wouldn't know how cool she is.

Mrs. Hall walks out of the class. "Sarah, are you alright?"

She shakes her head as she lowers it back into her hands.

"Do you want to go to the nurse? Maybe see if your mom or dad can pick you up?"

She keeps her head down but nods.

I look up at Mrs. Hall. "Can I take her to the nurse?"

She nods. I stand first and hold out my hand to her. Sarah sniffles and slowly reaches her hand up to mine. I help her up.

"Thanks," she whispers.

"It's cool."

She stops, turning to look at me. "Not just for walking with me." She pauses and looks down at her feet, then takes a deep breath before looking back up at me. "For not wanting me to see it."

We start walking towards the nurse's office. "Is it okay if I come over again today? I know we're done with the project, but I can bring you your book bag."

"You don't have to do that."

We reach the door. The nurse looks up at us. "I want to."

She smiles just a little bit. "Okay."

She's spinning her ring again. She always does that when she's nervous. Why is she nervous?

"You okay?" I ask.

Her chestnut eyes lift from her math homework and meet mine. She nods before dropping her eyes back to her work. She wore a tank top under her shirt at school today, I don't even know until we get to her house and she takes the top shirt off. I'm not sure if I've ever really noticed her shoulders before.

I tilt my American History book so it looks like I'm reading the chapter I'm supposed to be reading. Instead of reading, I watch her. Her hair is pulled back, a couple of pieces hanging around her face. My fingers itch to tuck each strand behind her ears. She has small dragonfly studs in them. I was with her when she bought them.

She couldn't decide between the dragonflies or elephant ones. I offered to get them both for her, but she wouldn't let me. The only gift she's ever accepted was that ring she's still spinning. I start to look at her hands and almost drop my book when she leans forward. She's across the coffee table from me; her tank top is loose, and I can see her bra. It's white with a lace trim. I gnaw on the corner of my lip.

The skin peeking out over the top of each cup is driving me crazy. I want to touch her. I pull my eyes away from her breasts feeling like a perv. My penance is short lived. I can't look away. Oblivious to my stare, I watch her chest rise and fall with each breath she takes. When my dick starts getting hard, I shift in my chair and cover my crotch with my forearm.

A throat clears from the doorway, and we both look up.

"Hey, Brian," Sarah says cheerfully.

"Sup," he answers her, but his eyes stay on me.

Shit. He must have seen me looking down her top. I wonder how long he's been standing there.

"Hey, Will. Can I talk to you for a sec?" He sounds calm, but he looks pissed.

Fuck. Sarah looks confused, but I shrug and stand. Grateful his presence killed my semi, I follow him into the kitchen.

He opens the fridge and takes out a soda, leaning back against the door as he opens it. After a quick pull from the can, he sets it on the kitchen table and rubs his hand across his chin. I stand awkwardly across the table from him waiting for him to say something.

"Will, can you bring me a soda once you're done?" Sarah shouts from the family room.

Brian smiles at the sound of her voice, his head tilted in the direction of it.

"Ah, sure," I reply.

His smile turns into a smirk as he looks at me. "I saw you."

My eyes drop to the kitchen table. I don't know how to respond to that.

"Did you like what you saw?"

There is no way I'm answering that question.

"Look at me."

Shit. Brian's always been cool to me. He's a senior this year. Sarah and I are both freshmen. I look up at him, wondering if I'm about to get my ass kicked.

"That's my baby sister, dude."

I'm not sure what to say so I nod. That seems to work because his expression relaxes.

He pulls a chair out and sits down. "Do you like her?"

"She's my best friend." I answer honestly.

He looks up at the ceiling. "I know that, Will, but do you like her as more than a friend?"

I look back down. "I don't know."

"Then you need to look elsewhere until you figure that out."

I nod and push off from the counter to head back into the family room.

"Will."

I turn back. He's standing now and reaching into the fridge to pass me the soda Sarah asked for.

"Thanks," I mumble, taking it.

Sarah is looking up at me when I walk back into the room. I carefully set her drink down in front of her, making sure my eyes go nowhere near her chest.

"What did Brian want?"

HER

"I wanted to know if he was going to try out for JV lacrosse," Brian answers for me before heading upstairs.

"Why couldn't he ask you that in here?" she asks, lifting one brow.

"Um, he didn't want to disturb you."

She gives me a look that says yeah right. "So are you?"

I'm confused. "Am I what?"

"Going to try out?"

"Maybe. Not sure."

"I think you should." She smiles up at me.

I nod and slump back down into my chair. I need to get through this chapter, but even after my talk with Brian, I'm finding it hard to concentrate. Do I like Sarah? I know I like her. She's my best friend, but I think I might like her more than that.

What sucks is she's so different from other girls at our school. With them, it's easy to tell how they feel about me. They look me with silly grins and giggle or blush if I talk to them. Sarah doesn't do that. If anything, she rolls her eyes and makes fun of me instead. What's the point of liking her as more than a friend if she doesn't like me that way back?

I slam my book shut, and she jumps.

"Sorry," I pause. "My head just isn't into homework."

She sets her pencil down. "What do you want to do?"

I feel like moving around. "Basketball?"

She shrugs. "Okay, I'm going to change first."

I pack all of my stuff into my backpack and set it on the bench by their front door. Sarah comes back downstairs a minute later wearing some loose, track pants with stripes running down the sides and an old t-shirt. I've seen that shirt on her before. It's just been awhile. I don't think it pulled that tightly across her chest the last time she wore it. I look away quickly, wondering where Brian is. I follow Sarah outside to their shed, and she rummages around until she finds the ball.

She passes it to me. "Think it needs air?"

I try to dribble it before nodding. She turns and starts looking for the bike pump. Once she finds it, she passes me the needle. Once it's ready, she starts pumping, and I can't take my eyes off of her. Each time she pumps it, her boobs push together. She's straining to get it as full as she can.

For my own sanity, I take the pump from her to finish it off. She rolls her eyes at me. Thank God she can't read my mind. Once the ball is pumped, we walk two streets over to a park with some basketball hoops. There's an open one. Sarah grabs the ball from me and takes a shot.

"Swish," she grins, her hand still up in the air.

I collect the ball and hold it under my arm. "What do you want to play?"

"I don't care. You pick."

I'm going to hell. "One on one?"

HER

"Sure."

I'm closer to the basket so I bounce pass the ball to her. She dribbles to the left, but I'm right there. She turns around so her back is to me and tries to push me back closer to the basket. I let her, only half-heartedly trying to get the ball from her. She turns and shoots, but the ball bounces off the rim. I grab it and dribble out to half court.

She smirks at me, legs wide, ready to go whatever direction I go. Instead of faking either direction, I head straight towards her. She sucks at blocking, and I'm taller than her. I hold the ball above my head and laugh as she tries to jump up and knock it out of my hands. Sarah glares up at me and stomps on my foot, hard.

"Fuck." I drop the ball and grab my foot.

She just laughs and runs after the ball.

"You play dirty," I snap when she makes her basket.

She ignores me and does a celebration dance. Last thing I need to see is Sarah jumping up and down in a tight shirt. I can't take my eyes off her, though. Maybe basketball was a bad idea. I ignore how cute she looks and try and think of her as one of the guys. Even if I liked her it wouldn't matter. She only likes me as a friend. I try and think about other girls at school. I think a couple sophomores like me. Maybe I'll ask one of them out.

When we get to twenty-one, we stop and walk back to her house. She's breathing heavy and her shirt is clinging to her back.

She pours us both cups of water from the sink. I watch as she gulps hers down, a thin trail of water running down her chin. When she finishes her cup, she gives me a wide smile. Her eyes are bright, her entire expression impish. I wish I had my camera. I follow her back out to the family room. I still don't feel like doing homework.

"Let's watch a movie."

"Sure. You pick."

I walk over to their DVDs and flip through them before settling on Saving Private Ryan "This good?" I ask, holding it up.

"That works. Want popcorn?"

I smile, and she stands. Halfway to the kitchen, she looks back at me. "Should we ask Brian—"

"Ask Brian what?" he says, walking into the family room.

I hold up the movie.

"Nah, I'm heading out." He turns towards the kitchen. "Sarah, tell Mom I won't be home for dinner."

"Where are you going?" she asks.

He grins. "Got a date."

"With who?"

He laughs. "Daniella Derrick."

My mouth drops. Every guy in our school is hot for double Ds. Sarah sees my expression and rolls

HER

her eyes before turning around towards the kitchen. That probably wasn't a smart move.

I peek around the corner to see if Sarah is there before turning back towards Brian. "Man, she's hot."

Brian smirks at me for a minute, making me sweat, until he grins and says, "Yeah, she is."

He turns and leaves, and I get the DVD started. I wait to press play until Sarah is back in the room with the popcorn. She is a total bowl hog, always has been. The only way I ever get any popcorn is if she tosses it for me to catch. I've gotten pretty good at it. Sarah covers her eyes when they land in Normandy. When we watch movies like this, it's my job to let her know when it's safe to look again. I sit at one end of the couch, her feet in my lap. We're still like this when her mom gets home.

"Hey, kids. How was school?"

We both groan, which makes her smile. She makes sure we've both finished our homework before going into the kitchen to start dinner. I lie about reading my history chapter. I'll do it before I go to bed. Her mom doesn't ask if I'm staying for dinner anymore. It's a given. Sarah gets up to let her know Brian won't be home for dinner. When she gets back, she smiles before putting her feet back in my lap. I almost jump when her foot brushes against my dick. I start thinking about things that turn me off: our principal, Brian kicking my ass, the Energizer bunny.

2

I just got asked out. I wasn't sure what to do so I said okay. Part of me feels like I'm being unfaithful to Sarah, but that's crazy.

Her name is Karen Bishop. She's a sophomore. Technically, since it's the last week of school, she's almost a junior. I'm about to go out with a junior. One of her friends was standing next to her when she asked. They both just stared at me until I answered her. She's pretty, but it's not like I even know her that well. I just panicked and said yes. I haven't told Sarah yet. She has to stay after to take a science test she missed. I stay after and hang out in the gym so I can ride the late bus home with her. I'll tell her then.

I'm waiting by her locker when she walks up after her retest. She doesn't look happy.

"How'd your test go?" I ask cautiously.

She pauses, her face relaxing. "Fine. It went fine." She pauses and looks down at her feet. "So when were you going to tell me about Karen Bishop?"

My mouth drops. Karen asked me out after sixth period. How had Sarah already heard about it?

She reads my mind. "Oh, Tracy Parlond told me before our retest." She's trying to sound like she doesn't care, but I can tell she's annoyed.

"I was going to tell you. It just happened." She shuts her locker, and I follow her down the hall. "Are you annoyed at me?"

She stops, her mouth open.

"Well?" I just want her to admit it.

She rolls her eyes. "I just thought, as your best friend, that I would hear it from you."

"I haven't seen you since it happened, until now." I bump her shoulder with mine, and she smiles.

Makes me want to pull my camera out and take her picture. She hates pictures of herself, though. She thinks she looks weird in them. We make our way out to the bus circle.

After we're seated, I ask. "Well, what do you think?"

She spins her ring, her eyes on it before looking up at me "She's very pretty."

"She is," I agree.

"I've never talked to her." She hesitates. "She seems nice, though."

I nod.

"So what are you guys going to do?"

"Going to the movies. Want to come?"

She bumps her shoulder into mine. "Dork. You didn't just invite me to tag along on your date."

Whoops. "Probably not a good idea."

"Probably," she agrees. At least she doesn't seem mad at me anymore.

"How do you think you did on the retest?"

"Good, which means I probably failed it." She spins her ring then laughs. "How many more days 'til summer break?"

"Not many. I can't wait. Plus, only six more months 'til I can get my license."

She rolls her eyes. It pisses her off that I'm turning sixteen four months before her, so I remind her every chance I get. When we get to her house Brian is already camped out in the family room watching Law and Order reruns. Sarah doesn't like that show so we go hang out in her room.

I'm trying to conjugate verbs for Spanish when she asks me if I'm nervous about my date.

I shut my Spanish book with my spiral notebook in it, saving my spot, before I answer. "I don't want to do anything embarrassing, but it's a movie so it's not like I have to talk a lot."

"How are you guys getting there?"

I grin. "She has a car. Cool, right?"

Sarah just rolls her eyes and doesn't say anything after that. What the hell? Why doesn't she think its cool Karen has a car? I look up when she stands.

"Want a snack?"

I get up and follow her down the stairs to their kitchen. She pops some popcorn while I make us root beer floats. She's in front of me, holding the bowl as we walk up the stairs. Her ass is right at eye level, I can't take my eyes off of it. She doesn't wear tight stuff like most girls at our school. The t-shirt she's wearing is baggy but not long enough to cover her ass.

She's wearing black soccer shorts, and every step she takes, they pull tighter to one side. I'm not paying attention and almost trip. She must notice me stumble because she's laughing at me as we walk back into her room. Bet she wouldn't be if she knew why I almost tripped.

We finish our homework just as Brian is leaving for his part-time job at the mall. We talk him into dropping us off at the pool on his way to work. Brian lets me borrow one of his old suits. Sarah leaves a note for her mom letting her know where we'll be. When we get to the pool, we sit with some kids from our school. Sarah's the only girl wearing a one-piece. She's also the only girl who will play sharks and minnows.

She hates it when I'm a shark. I always ignore everyone else and go right after her. I swim faster than she does, so I sneak up on her and pull her by her ankle. She looks like she wants to kill me every time she comes up sputtering. It's great.

We stay for a couple hours before walking back to her house. It's not a long walk, but my legs feel like Jello. By next summer, I'll be driving. Then we can go to the amusement park or the mall.

HER

Mrs. Miller is already making dinner when we get back. I change in their downstairs bathroom and put Brian's suit and the towel I used on their back deck to dry while Sarah goes upstairs. I'm hanging out with her mom in the kitchen when she comes back down, already in her pajamas. She shrugs when I give her a look.

"I'm lazy. What?" she snaps.

"Sarah be nice and set the table."

When her mom isn't looking, she rolls her eyes and reaches for the plates. I don't know why she's annoyed. Her mom is great. I wish my mom was as cool; instead, she just doesn't seem to notice me at all. I take the plates from her to help. She grins and turns around to grab forks and knives.

Once the table is set, we go hang out in the den. Her dad comes home not long after. He pops his head in the door to say hello to us before heading back to the kitchen. I can hear them talking in there about work and their days. Mrs. Miller mentions a movie she wants to see. He asks if she'd like him to take her tonight. It's quiet, and I know she's kissing him.

I look over at Sarah. I know she worries sometimes that the kids at school think her house isn't big enough or the car her dad drives isn't fancy enough. I wonder if she gets how lucky she is. How most of the kids we go to school with would kill to have parents as laidback and cool as hers. The difference is they care.

My mom seems spaced out all the time and my dad works all the time so he doesn't have to deal. I think of the Millers as more of my parents than my actual mom and dad.

After dinner, Mrs. Miller drives me home. Sarah comes along, and we both sit in the back and listen to the radio. Sarah teases me about Karen. To anyone else, I'd play it off like it was no big deal, but with Sarah I can't.

"So what do you think you'll do after the movie?" she asks.

I shake my head. "I have no clue. I don't even know if she'll want to hang out."

She gives me a look. "Of course she'll want to hang out. Are you going to kiss her?"

"Maybe." I admit. "It'd be cool to kiss a sophomore."

"Maybe?" she questions. "Do you think she's pretty?"

I picture her face. "I guess."

Her mouth drops, and she reaches out to push my shoulder. "You guess? Will, she is one of the prettiest girls at our school." She sounds surprised.

That right there is one of the coolest things about Sarah. I know so many girls who can't admit another girl is pretty, like saying it somehow makes them less. Or they'll make some backhanded compliment like, 'yeah she's pretty, if you're into that.' What does 'that' even mean? Who wouldn't be into pretty? With the exception of Sarah, I don't understand girls at all. Half of the time, I'm not even sure if I understand her too. Even Karen, who I do think is really pretty. I don't understand why she asked me out. I'm flattered, but I don't even know her or have any classes with her. I've had girls ask me out before, just never one I didn't really know.

Sarah's looking at me, waiting for me to say something. I just lift my hands and shrug. I know she is cool to talk to, but this isn't the kind of stuff I want to share.

"Thanks. Mrs. M," I say, grabbing my backpack and tilting my chin toward Sarah. She gives me a half wave and moves to the front seat.

"So, how was it?" she asks quietly.

I roll onto my side so the phone is tucked under my ear. "Mmmm. I don't know. Not great. We didn't really talk at all," I admit.

She laughs in my ear. "Will, you're not supposed to talk at a movie."

"I know that." I snap. "I mean when we were in her car and before the movie. Then after the movie we got milkshakes."

"Oh. Did you talk about anything?" she asks.

I turn so I'm on my back and press speaker phone. "She told me about her pet bird."

I start to say more, but she cuts me off. "Am I on speakerphone?"

I pause. She hates speakerphone. "Maybe."

"Will, take me off of speakerphone," she orders.

"Fine." I grumble, lifting the phone back to my ear. "Better?"

"Much, just don't ever do it again." She pauses. I can hear her holding back a laugh. "A pet bird? Sounds thrilling."

I smile. "Very. I think she was bored too. Don't see a second date in my future." I'm not disappointed.

"So." She seems to hesitate. I'm about to say something when she continues. "No goodnight kiss?"

"No kiss," I answer.

She makes a click sound with her mouth. "Too bad you already picked out baby names."

Sometimes Sarah says straight up crazy things. "Do what?"

She sighed. "Just trying to be funny. Ignore me."

I laugh. "That was supposed to be funny? You seriously need to work on your material."

"Oh, it's on." She scoffs.

"What, like Donkey Kong?" I finish, laughing.

HER

Our freshman year is finally over, we're officially sophomores. I haven't gone out with Karen again, and that's cool. I have three goals for this summer: get my learner's permit, hang out at the pool, and do as little as humanly possible.

Sarah is babysitting a kid named Colin on her block for the summer. He's eight so at least she won't have to be changing diapers or anything, and he loves the pool so I can still hang out with her there. My dad has been too busy with work to teach me how to drive. I was bummed until Mr. Miller offered to teach me along with Sarah on the weekends. Today is our first lesson.

He drives us over to the high school. They have a big parking lot, and other than a couple of cars belonging to people running on the track, it's deserted. We both sit in the back on the way over. Sarah is terrified. Me? I can't wait.

He turns to look at us. "So who's going first?"

Sarah looks at me with a look that's clearly meant to tell me to go first. Fine. I'll bite. "I'll go, sir." I grin.

"Alright, William, Sarah. Out of the car." We glance at each other, confused.

He pops the hood and explains stuff like checking the oil, coolant, and transmission fluid. He has us walk around the car and look at the tires before taking out a gauge to show us how to check if they need air or not. After all of that, he has me sit in the driver's seat and adjust the seat and mirrors to where they feel comfortable. He and Sarah are still outside of the car. He has her stand off to the side before getting in.

"Now, William. Check all your mirrors. Do you see Sarah?"

I do what he asks. I check the rear and side mirrors, but I can't see her in any of them. I have to turn my head and look out the window to see her.

"That, young man, is your blind spot. Before you ever think about turning or changing lanes, remember to look first." He looks at her. "Got that, young lady?"

"Blind spot. Check." She says seriously.

He shouts for Sarah to get back in the car, muttering that Mrs. Miller will kill him if I run her over. They both laugh while I internally reject the idea of anything ever happening to her. I don't think I could deal with that. After everyone is buckled, he lets me start the car. This is the coolest feeling ever. Closest I've ever come to doing something like this is the one time Kyle Nelson let me ride his scooter around the block. My mom saw me when she was driving home from work. She was not happy about it and forbid me from ever going on another one.

The gear shifter is in the middle. He has me practice moving it from park, to reverse, to drive, and back, all with my foot on the brake. It's weird how you use one foot to drive even though there are two pedals. Wouldn't it just make more sense to use both feet?

It doesn't help that I can see Sarah from the rearview mirror. She's covering her mouth with both hands at my questions. I'm so giving her shit when it's her turn. He has me take my foot off the brake. The car moves forward slowly. It feels too fast. I glance over at him, and he nods, telling me I'm doing fine. He has me turn the steering wheel to get an idea of how far I need to move it for the car to turn. When he has me give it a bit of gas, we all jerk forward.

"Next time just ease onto it," he says calmly.

My eyes flick to Sarah's in the rear mirror. I'm nervous, thinking maybe I scared her.

She just shakes her head and sticks her tongue out at me.

I take a couple laps around the parking lot before he has me park it so Sarah can have her turn. He doesn't pop the hood again or have us look at the tires since she's already seen it. He does do the thing where I'm now standing in her blind spot.

Once she starts the car and gives it a bit of gas, she's a natural. I chew on the corner of my lip. Somehow, I assumed I would be the better driver. I kill her in Mario Cart on a regular basis. Her eyes meet mine through the rear view mirror, and she lifts her eyebrows. Fuck. She is so going to give me shit for this.

After she parks, Christ, between the lines on the first try, Mr. Miller takes us for ice cream. I sit quietly on the way over, waiting for the first dig.

She elbows me, her eyes bright. "That was so cool."

I shrug and feel like shit when her face falls.

"What's wrong?" She gets this little wrinkle right between her eyebrows.

I look out my window, depressed, before looking back at her. "I thought I'd be better at it."

She starts spinning her ring. That means she's trying to think of something to say to make me feel better, which means I wasn't imagining it. I drove like shit.

"You weren't that bad," she grins.

Now I feel worse. "Thanks, Sarah. Translation: I sucked ass." I cringe and glance at Mr. Miller to see if he heard me. If he did, he's not acting like it.

"You did not suck ass. Are you just pissed that I did better? 'Cause that sucks ass if you are. This isn't a competition." She crosses her arms over her chest.

Awesome. Damage control time. "That isn't what I was saying. My birthday is before yours. It's just freaking me out." I look at her to see if she believes me.

She leans over, putting her head on my shoulder. "You don't have to worry. My dad will totally take us out again. Right, dad?"

HER

He grunts a response as he pulls into the parking lot of the ice cream place. Sarah sits up and is out of the car before I can even acknowledge the fact that I miss her head on my shoulder. Sarah and I both get chocolate dipped waffle cones while Mr. Miller gets a plain old cake cone. We look at him like he's crazy, but neither of us rag him for it since he's buying.

3

"Hey come outside."

"What are you doing here?" She looks at me sideways.

I grab her hand and tug her up off of the couch. "I want you to see something."

"Hang on." She grumbles. "Let me find my shoes."

Once she has them on, Sarah follows me to her front door. Before I open it, I spin around so I'm facing her and cover her eyes with my hand. She reaches up to steady herself, placing one of her hands on my forearm. I glance down at her hand, wishing there wasn't a jacket keeping her skin from mine.

"Really? You have to cover my eyes? We're going to be late for school, and I haven't had breakfast," she huffs.

"Don't worry. We have time. Besides, I know you'll cheat and peek."

She smiles because she knows I'm right. I snake my other hand behind me to open the door and walk backwards out it, pulling her with me. Once we're off her front stoop and standing in front of her driveway, I move my hand.

"A car!" she exclaims. "You got a car. It's gorgeous," she gushes while I grin, watching her.

She walks all the way around it before she tries the front passenger door. When it doesn't open, she smirks at me.

"Now what do we say?" I tease.

"Don't be a tool and open the door Will," she says, tugging on the door handle.

I unlock the doors, and she climbs in. I walk around to the driver side and sit next to her.

"A sunroof," she shrieks pressing the button and looking at me when it doesn't work.

"The car needs to be on, Einstein." I joke, putting the key in the ignition. "Wanna ride to school?"

"Hell yeah," she says, pulling her seatbelt on.

"Forgetting something?" I ask.

"Oh crap," she grunts, letting go of the seatbelt and jumping out of the car. I wait for her as she grabs her stuff for school. I'm used to this by now. She always forgets stuff.

"Does this mean my days of riding the bus are over?" she asks, sliding back in after grabbing her backpack.

I nod. As I back out, she presses the button to open the sunroof.

"It's December, Sarah." I laugh as she pouts.

She shrugs it off, pressing the button to close it before she starts messing with the buttons on the stereo and climate controls. "It's still badass. Did your parents get it for you?"

I nod. It was a total shock. My dad is usually walking out the door when I wake up. Instead, when I went to leave, he and my mom were waiting for me at the bottom of the stairs with a set of keys. It took me a minute to realize I wasn't dreaming the dark blue, four-door Jetta with a giant red bow on top parked in our driveway. My parents followed me outside. I managed to hug and thank my dad before he hurried off to work. I had gone to do the same for my mom, but she had already gone back inside the house.

On the way to school, I hit a drive thru Starbucks and get Sarah a scone and a latte.

She cups her drink in her hands, lifting it to her nose to smell it.

"You know you're my favorite person ever." Her chocolate eyes lock on mine.

I gulp. "I know." She's mine.

"And here you are, buying me breakfast on your birthday."

"It's no big deal," I argue.

She nods. "It is a big deal. Promise me we'll be best friends forever."

I laugh. "Done."

"Good." She pulls a piece off of the scone and pops it into her mouth.

"This is really good. Want a bite?"

I open my mouth for to her feed me. She breaks off another small piece and sets it between my lips, her fingertips barely grazing them. My eyes widen. Shit. I'm getting turned on. It's only a semi, so as long as I concentrate on other things, it'll go back down.

"Can I take you out to the movies tonight for your birthday?"

I nod, not looking at her.

"Want another bite?"

I shake my head. Get it together, I tell myself. She's your best friend, and it just isn't going to happen. After I've parked, we walk in together at the entrance by the cafeteria, away from the bus drop off loop.

She elbows me to get my attention. "I'll be your very best friend if you give me rides so I never, ever have to ride the bus again."

I smirk at her. "You already are my very best friend. Got a better offer?"

I hold back a laugh when I see the look she gives me.

"William Price," she says. "If I had a car, I would do it for you."

I bump my shoulder into hers and laugh as it knocks her a couple steps away. She catches back up to me and flicks her leg up to kick my ass.

"Yes, I will give you rides," I concede as we reach her locker.

She gives me a cheesy grin and shrugs off her coat. Underneath, she's wearing one of my old hoodies. I poke my finger into a hole forming on the side. She smacks my hand away, laughing.

"You might have to retire this one."

Her eyes are wide as they snap to mine. "But I love it."

I chew on the side of my lip and shake my head at her. "You love my old UGA hoodie?"

She hugs herself and nods solemnly. She has most of the ones I've outgrown, and a couple I haven't. They swim on her, but she doesn't care. Neither do I. I like how she looks in them.

We head to my locker next, then split to go to our homerooms. We only have one class and the same lunch period this year. We picked the same electives, thinking we would end up together, but it hadn't worked out. The one class we do have together is gym, which is second period. She waits for me after first period.

Her class is closer to the gym, so I meet her there every day and we walk together. The entrances to the locker rooms are on opposite sides of the gym. I veer off and go get changed. We meet back up in the gym, now sporting our Decatur P.E. uniforms: navy blue shorts and gray t-shirts. Our gym teacher walks out with an extension cord and a boombox.

"Who's ready to dance?" he asks.

A collective groan is his response. Sarah is standing next to me. I glance down at her and lift my eyebrows. She nods. Assuming we're allowed to pick our own partners, we're set. Not that it matters. The first dance we learn is a line dance. Not my thing. I try and keep from laughing at Sarah, though. I'm somewhat getting it; she is not. Not even close. She just looks at me and grins, playing off her mistakes with style, busting out the macarena every once and a while.

Coach gives us five to go get water. We race, and she gets there first, but only because I let her win. Her hair is pulled back in a ponytail, little pieces falling out around her face. I feel pervy watching her lean over, mouth open as she drinks. She cups some water in her hand and lets it drip down the back of her neck.

"Close your mouth before you catch flies." She laughs at me, flicking water in my direction.

I blink, clamping my mouth shut, and ease myself between her and the fountain. She huffs at me, but she was hogging the water and my throat is feeling especially parched. She waits for me, and we walk back to the center of the gym together. I glance at my watch. Only ten more minutes until we're released to hit the showers. Coach sees me look at my watch then looks over at the line of kids still waiting to get water before releasing us early.

Sarah jogs off to the girls' locker room while I stand transfixed watching her ass. Once she's out of

HER

sight, I move. Our showers are cubicle-styled. If I wasn't at school, I'd probably be rubbing one off right now.

I don't know what my problem is. Just thinking about her is messing with my mind. It's impossible to take a shower and not touch your dick. I purposely try to avoid lingering there because if anyone catches me I will never live it down. It just feels good, and it's like my hands have a mind of their own.

I'm waiting for her. Her wet hair leaves spots on the shoulder of my hoodie. I love the way her conditioner smells, tropical, like mangos. A lot of girls at our school like the flowery smelling crap. I'm not a fan. I pause, waiting for her while she twists her hair up into a bun.

Lacrosse practice kicked my ass today. I fucking hate suicides, and coach had us do a ton. Sprint, then drop and do twenty pushups. Over and over again. I'm dragging as I head to shower and change. The guys are talking about some girl when I walk in. Bravo sees me and tells Todd to shut up. The vibe just seems weird.

"What's up?" I ask.

Bravo just shakes his head and looks away.

I glance over at Todd and ask again.

He shrugs. "I was just wondering if anyone else saw what Sarah Miller was wearing today."

Some guys snicker but stop when they see my glare. "Why would any of you care about what she was wearing?"

I'm thinking back to what she was wearing earlier. I'm pretty sure it was just jeans and a hoodie, my hoodie.

He leans in like he's got a secret. "Her nipples were" is all he gets out before I punch him.

He goes down hard and holds his jaw while I get right in his face. "Not cool, man. You do not talk about her like that. Ever. Got me?"

"What's going on here?" Coach booms, coming around the corner.

Bravo tugs me back. "Nothing, Coach, Todd just slipped and fell." He looks at Todd. "Right, Todd?"

Todd looks up at me and nods. Coach tells him to ice his face and tells the rest of us to hit the showers. I'm pissed, fucking asshole talking about her like that, like it's okay. It drives me crazy knowing other guys even think about her.

Sarah doesn't seem to think of me as anything other than a friend. I know I'm attracted to her, but there is no way I'm making a move on her. I can't risk ruining our friendship. She is the one constant in my life.

My parents are oblivious. I bombed a science test, and my teacher, Mr. Norman made me bring a copy of it home for one of them to sign. I put it on the kitchen counter, and it sat there for three days before I just scribbled my mom's name and turned it back in.

This blonde girl at school has been flirting with me. I'm nervous about dating anyone, but she's pretty and it's not like I can ask Sarah out. Beginning of our junior year, I started dating this girl named Jen. She couldn't handle my friendship with Sarah.

Looking back, I can see her point. It had to have felt bad that I'd rather spend time with Sarah than her. When she gave me the ultimatum of choosing between them, she wasn't surprised when I didn't pick her.

This blonde, Jessica, doesn't seem to mind Sarah, so maybe it's worth a shot. She's in two of my classes. I only have lunch this year with Sarah. She doesn't have a car so I still drive her to and from school. Today, when we get to school, Jessica is waiting for me by my locker.

Sarah gives me a look before turning in the other direction and heading off to her first period. I watch her walk away. I gnaw on my lip, hoping she isn't annoyed at me.

When she turns the corner, I walk the rest of the way to my locker. "Hey," I say, not really sure what she wants.

"Hi, Will." She twirls a strand of her hair. "I was wondering if you wanted to hang out together this Friday?"

I look at her. It's Wednesday. I'm trying to remember if I'm supposed to be doing anything that night. There's a new movie Sarah wants to see, but we can always go see that on Saturday.

She's looking at me, waiting for me to reply. "I guess. What'd you want to do?"

She purses her lips to the side, and I have to admit she's pretty hot. She wears way more makeup than Sarah, and her clothes are tighter too. I'm not crazy about the makeup, but her legs look amazing. Sarah almost never wears dresses. The last time I think I saw her in one was her dad's last birthday. We all went out to dinner at this Italian place.

"We could go to Java Monkey. I heard they have a band play on Fridays. Then we can hang out at my house. My parents are out of town." She adds that last part quietly, looking up at me through her lashes.

Her house. I shut my locker and nod. "Sounds good. Do you want to meet there or—"

She doesn't let me finish. She steps closer to me. "Why don't you—" She presses her index finger into my chest. "Pick me up at seven."

We have the same first period and walk to class together. When we get there, it sucks that her desk isn't near mine. I like the attention. All through class, I watch her. A few times, she catches me. The last time she winks. That is hot. I tell Sarah about our date when we meet up for lunch.

Her mouth drops, and she crosses her arms over her chest. "I thought we were going to the movies."

"Don't be pissed. We can go Saturday." I steal the apple from her tray.

She raises her eyebrow and steals a corner of my brownie.

"Hey."

"Don't hate, apple thief." She points to my acquisition.

"I only wanted a bite," I say before handing it back to her.

"So did I," she returns, chomping into her apple.

Halfway through lunch, Sarah brings up Jessica. "So do you like her?"

I nervously chew on the side of my lip. "I don't know. She seems cool."

"What are you guys doing?"

"I'm not sure. I think we might go to Java Monkey and then hang out at her house." I try and play it off like it's not a big deal.

She starts coughing, and I thump her back. She catches her breath. "Sorry, a piece went down the wrong hole." Her voice sounds rough. She clears her throat. "So will her parents be there?"

I shake my head. "She said they are going to be out of town."

She looks down at her watch and jumps up. "I totally forgot. I have this thing. I have to go." Her voice sounds different.

I look at her. "What thing? Where are you going?"

She already has her food piled up onto her tray and is pulling the straps of her backpack up her arms. "It's nothing. I'll see you after school."

With that, she's gone. What just happened?

I stare at the now empty seat across from me. We always eat lunch together. If she had something going on, she would have told me before.

I'm in a room full of people, but I suddenly feel isolated. I glance around. It feels weird eating by myself. There are a group of girls checking me out from the table next to ours. No thank you. I look down at my tray. I've officially lost my appetite. I stand, get all my stuff together, and leave the cafeteria.

Why do girls have to be so confusing? I walk to my locker and get my stuff for the next two periods. Jessica is in my next class. I'm actually looking forward to seeing her. I get there early since I already ran by my locker. I'm sitting when she walks in. She smiles when she sees me, like a really big happy smile.

HER

I can't help but smile back. Her seat isn't next to me, but it's close. She carries a messenger bag instead of a backpack and hangs it on the back of her chair. The bell hasn't rung yet, so she walks over to me and half sits on my desk. Her ass is on my desk, right in front of me. I have to shift in my seat.

"Hi, Will."

She's wearing a button up shirt with a collar. There's a little space between two of the buttons. Holy shit, I can see her bra and a sliver of her breast. Fuck, I'm hard. I slip my hand into my pocket and press my dick flat against me, tucking it under the waistband of my boxers.

"Hey, Jessica." If she noticed my adjustment, she isn't letting on.

"I'm really looking forward to hanging out on Friday." God, the way she says 'really' makes my dick twitch.

I clear my throat. "Yeah, me too." I just about groan.

The bell rings, and she slides off my desk and walks back over to hers, her hips rocking back and forth. I almost feel guilty for the thoughts racing through my brain. I barely hear what Mrs. Tunstall is saying or writing on the board. All I can see is Jessica's white bra.

I blink when the bell rings. Jessica is waiting by her desk. I wonder if she's waiting for me. When she falls into step next to me, I know she is. Life is weird. I hardly know this girl, and now I can't stop thinking about her. She really seems to like me. It's just odd that we never really talked before.

We pause outside the door. "Which way?" I hold my hands up, thumbs pointing in either direction down the hall. She points left.

I frown. "I'm heading that way." I point right. My last period is almost across the hall, just a couple doors down.

She leans in and kisses my cheek. "I guess I'll see you around."

I tilt my head and watch her disappear into the sea of kids in the hallway before shaking my head and heading to my next class. I've been kissed before; I've even made out with a few girls. I just wasn't expecting her to do that, so I think it's hitting me harder.

I can't stop thinking about Friday night. It hits me in class why I never really hung out with her before. She was dating this guy, Brice. He moved away at the beginning of the year.

After school, I meet Sarah at her locker. "Where'd you have to go at lunch?"

She's looking for something, digging through a pile of papers that seems to be a permanent fixture at the bottom of her locker. It's funny. From this angle she looks almost headless. I pull my camera out of my bag and snap her picture. She pops her head out and glares. My camera is still out so I'm caught. I stick my tongue out at her and snap another picture. "Give me angry." I command.

Her mouth twitches, and I know she's trying not to laugh. "What about studious? Give me studious."

She raises one eyebrow. "Is this necessary?"

"Always." I reply. "So what are you looking for?"

"I have a paper due on Monday, and I can't find the handout that has the requirements on it." She sounds frustrated and makes a halfhearted flip through the stack again.

"Just ask your teacher for another one." It seems obvious.

"I can't." She groans, shutting her locker door and resting her forehead on it.

"Okay, drama, why not?" Her hair has fallen forward. All thoughts of Jessica leave me as my fingers itch to tuck those loose strands behind her ear. She is so cute when she's acting crazy, which happens a lot.

"Mr. Jones hates me." She tilts her chin to the side, forehead still on her locker, but somehow the movement exposes her eye. "Hates me."

I shake my head. "I'll bite. Why does he hate you?"

She turns around, presses her back to her locker and slides down it until she's sitting on the floor in front of it. She drops her head into her hands. It feels weird talking to her when she's on the ground, and I'm standing so I sit down next to her.

She lifts her head and pouts. "I had a complete brainfart in class last week and couldn't remember who wrote Hamlet." She pauses to sniffle. "So he goes off on this rant about our generation being too focused on TV and the internet and that our brains are wasting away. He hates me."

"I'm sure you could get a copy from someone in your class."

She blinks at me. "Why didn't I think of that? I'll call Justin and get it from him."

What? Justin who? She's going to call some guy. I try and think of the Justins in our class and which one she might be talking about. I don't know why it bugs me, but it does. Does she have his number already in her phone? Have they talked before?

"If he's still here, you can get it before we leave." I say, wanting to know who this guy is, and if she gets what she needs now, there will be no reason to call him later.

"Oh, I can just call him." She says, smirking at me.

"It's not a big deal. Or we can swing by his house on the way home." What am I saying?

She crooks one eyebrow up at me. "It's no big deal, Will. I don't even know why I was so freaked out."

HER

I stand. She reaches her hand up to me, and I pull her up easily. Too easily, our chests bump, and she blushes, backing away. I have to stop thinking about her that way. She's my best friend. She probably sees me as her brother.

Shit. Brian would kill if he knew what I was thinking about doing to his little sister right now. She's just always so covered up, less during the summer and when we go to the pool and stuff. She doesn't wear crazy baggy stuff either, except for when she wears my old hoodies, which she does a lot.

I just think about undressing her. If I don't stop thinking about it, I'll be pitching a tent for the drive home. She holds the door for me as we walk out. It's stuff like that. Shouldn't I be trying to hold the door for her? I just need to focus on a girl who seems to like me. I think back to Jessica kissing my cheek.

When we get to my car, I can't let the Justin thing go, it's like a scab I have to pick. "So, Justin who?"

It's a warm day for November, and her arm is already raised halfway to push the button to open the sunroof. "Huh?"

I suck in the corner of my lip and chew on it. "What Justin are you calling for the English stuff?"

She folds her arms over her chest. "Justin Lange. Why?"

I exhale, picturing him. He was a good four inches shorter than her and still had braces. I was worried it was Justin Thorpe, who I played lacrosse with and was a wannabe player. "No reason."

She purses her lips and taps the side of her chin. "I could call Justin Thorpe. He gave me his number last week."

I brake a little too hard at the stop sign, and we both jerk in our seats. "What?"

Her eyes are wide when she looks at me. "You're acting weird. Why are you making such a big deal about this?"

I look out the rear view mirror to avoid her eyes. "You didn't tell me some guy gave you his number." I pause and scratch the back of my head. "Why'd he give you his number?"

She rolls her eyes. "Not for what you're thinking. We're in a group together for Government. I also got Natalie Bruster and Connor Hanson's numbers. I have both Justins in my English class, so it doesn't really matter who I call."

I can't help myself. I hate the idea of her talking to Justin Thorpe. "I think you should call Justin Lange."

4

I glance over at Jessica. Why am I even with her? I wonder if she feels the same way. Whatever excitement I had for her left me about two months into our relationship. I think she's holding on because we fit the expectation everyone has for us.

God, even my mom likes her, which is strange. Maybe it's not Jessica, but her parents my mom really likes. Mr. Burton is some executive for a credit union in town. I didn't know she was shallow like that.

We haven't even had sex in a month. She keeps trying, but it just doesn't feel right. I think she fakes even liking me. I think I'm just filling the spot left by her ex. I wish she would break up with me, but then what? I go back to pining after Sarah. I'm pathetic.

"I'm going to take off," I say, standing.

"Are you going home?"

I know what she's really asking. Are you going over to Sarah's?

I shake my head. I'm not surprised she looks annoyed, but I'd rather hang out with Sarah than watch stupid shit with her while neither of us talk.

She doesn't even follow me out the door and walk me to my car.

When I get there, Sarah isn't even home. I should have called her. Mrs. M tells me to stay and hang out with her. I'm wearing an apron, helping her make dinner, when Brian and Sarah walk in. They just about collapse on each other, laughing at me in my Kiss the Cook apron. Mrs. M clucks at them as I pull it off and hang it back in the pantry.

"Thanks for helping me, Will." Mrs. Miller pats my shoulder, giving Sarah and Brian a look.

"Where were you guys?" I ask as we all walk into the den.

Sarah falls back onto the sofa and holds up her legs. "See my new kicks."

She wants me to look at her new sneakers, but it's her legs that have my full attention. I look away when Brian's eyes narrow.

"Cool," I say, sitting down.

Brian faces me. "So how's your girlfriend?"

I can't help but notice Sarah roll her eyes as she picks up the remote. "Fine,"

I've just talked Sarah into going to the movies with Jessica and me. "I'm thinking about breaking up with her." She doesn't say anything. "So do you think I should?"

HER

She looks away. Crap. I want to see her eyes. She tells me she shouldn't be giving anyone dating advice.

"I think I like someone else." What I can't say is, it's her.

Her eyes snap to mine. "Who?"

I'm too chickenshit to tell her.

"Who is she?" she asks again.

I know it drives her crazy when she doesn't know. I shake my head. "I don't want to say. I don't think she likes me like that."

She doesn't say anything for the longest time. "Then she doesn't deserve you."

That's gotta be a good sign. I feel like pushing her up against the locker and kissing her, but I panic and put her in a headlock instead and start walking toward the door. She bats at my arm and cusses me out. It's awesome.

She's so cute when she's pissed off. I'm almost to the door when she gets real quiet. I look down at her just in time to watch her tongue flick out and slide up the inside of my upper arm. Stunned, I relax my arm right away and just stare at her dumbfounded. I'm unable to get the feel of her warm, wet tongue out of my head. She stretches her neck and sticks it back out at me.

"I can't believe you just licked my arm," I stammer.

When she tells me I deserved it, I let her know I'm so going to get her and chase her out the side door to the parking lot. She's screaming, but she's still fast and makes it to my car before I can catch her. We both drop our bags and stare at each other across my car, panting. Fuck, this is turning me on.

I'm not going to catch her if she sees me coming. I crouch down and slowly make my way around the car. She's hip to what I'm doing a second too late. I grab her, tossing her over my shoulder and run over to the field just past the parking lot. I flop her onto the grass, cringing, thinking that maybe I could have been more gentle. I sit on her, my legs on either side of her.

God, she's beautiful. All laid out, underneath me. Her brown hair is fanned out behind her, and her chest is rising and falling. It's her eyes that kill me. They're wild. She tries to buck me off, and I laugh when she confesses she has to pee and begs me not to tickle her. Shit, I don't want to make her piss herself. While that would be funny, she'd have to sit in my car afterward. I chew on my lip while I think about what to do to her.

Then I have it. "Deal."

She gasps when I lower my face to hers. We're almost nose to nose. "Doesn't mean that I won't still have my revenge." I breathe, trying not to dwell on how good she feels under me.

Her mouth is open. Her lips are right there. If I just lower my face one more inch, I can kiss her. It takes everything I have not to, especially when I see her eyes start to flutter shut. But, I'm already moving. Shit. Did she want me to kiss her? I lick the side of her face, from her chin to her temple then pull back to see her reaction.

Holy shit, it's priceless. I fall off of her and laugh, the almost kiss forgotten. She pushes at me and jumps up, marching over to my car. She's pissed, which sucks, but the look on her face almost makes it worth it. I'm trying not to laugh, I am. It's just that every time I look at her, I start all over again.

I pull her into a hug. She promptly stomps on my foot. I hold on to her even though that hurt like hell and kiss the top of her head before I let go. We're in my car and already halfway to her house; she's still pissed.

"Wanna press the button?" I grin, knowing it's her weakness.

She snorts.

"Well if you don't want to, I will." I say, lifting my hand.

I know she's forgiven me when she knocks my hand out of the way, saying "No, I'll press it."

When we get to her house, she races to the bathroom. I feel like being a tool so I wait for her just outside the door. She rolls her eyes at me, and I grin. God, I love her.

Shit, I *love* her.

I follow her into the kitchen and hang out while she makes popcorn. We go into the den to watch TV. My phone starts to ring. I almost ignore it when I see it's Jessica, but she'll just call back until I answer.

"Hey."

Sarah mouths 'who is it' and I mouth back 'Jessica' while Jessica is going on about this movie we're supposed to go see. She asks me if Sarah's still going with us. I tell her yes, and she replies that she has someone she wants to set her up with. "Hell no" is all I can think.

I glance over at Sarah. I don't want some guy dating her. "You didn't have to do that." Jessica argues in my ear while Sarah just sits there, looking confused. When Jessica tells me who, I say, "But I don't even think she likes him."

Jessica wants to know why I would say that and to ask Sarah. I look over at her. She's messing with her phone. She looks up at me as I hold the phone to my chest. "Jessica invited Kyle to come to the movies as your—" I hesitate. "Um, date." I spit the last word, hating the way it tastes.

Her eyes widen. I keep going. "I can just tell her you don't like him, and he doesn't have to come."

Her brows come together. "Kyle Nelson?"

I nod, hoping she'll say no.

"I'm okay going with Kyle," she says.

What the fuck?

After I hang up with Jessica, I stare at her, wondering if she might actually like him, knowing it would kill me if she did.

HER

Finally, it gets to her. "What?"

"I didn't know you liked Kyle," I admit, even though it's killing me.

She shrugs. "He's okay, I guess. I've never really hung out with him. Besides, I hate being the third wheel to you and whatever girl you end up dating. Maybe it'd be nice to have someone too."

"You never feel like a third wheel to me." Honestly, I'd rather it was just us, but I can't tell her that.

She rolls her eyes and flips onto her slide, stretching her feet out and onto my lap. I rest my hands on her calves. I have to fight the urge to rub them; her legs are soft and smooth and *in my lap*. I glance over at her. The way her shorts shifted when she turned, I can see right up them. Holy shit, I can see one rounded, beautiful (damnit, I'm getting hard) ass cheek.

My mouth waters, and I blurt. "Are you wearing underwear?"

Her face snaps to mine. "Excuse me?"

I can't shut up. Why did I say anything? "I can totally see your butt cheek."

She presses the back of her shorts down, and I lose my view. "Yes, I'm wearing underwear."

I look at her hand, still pressing her shorts to her skin and shake my head, picturing her ass. "It didn't look like it."

She notices the direction of my eyes. "Stop looking at my butt."

"Who's looking at your butt?"

Oh shit. We both look up as Brian walks in. Shit. Shit. Shit.

"Will is." Sarah says, throwing me under the bus.

He is absolutely going to kick my ass. Shit. I can't even try to defend the fact that I have a raging hard on. Fuck. I don't want to look like a bitch and cringe. His eyes are on mine as he walks across the room. He doesn't stop when he passes me on his way to the recliner on the other side of the sofa, but he does cuff the top of my head. Hard. He stops before sitting and points at me, then Sarah, then back at him. I nod, message received loud and fucking clear I think, while I rub my head. Shit, that hurt like hell.

Sarah pulls a blanket off the back of the couch and covers her ass with it. Brian doesn't stay long, not liking what we're watching. As soon as he leaves, we look at each other and crack up.

"Holy shit, I thought he was going to kick my ass there for a second," I admit once I'm done laughing.

She's still laughing. "How's your head?"

Not smart to tease the guy who has your feet in his lap, "You think that's funny?"

I reach past her and move the popcorn to the coffee table and then grab her ankles in one hard grip as I tickle her feet. She bucks like a wild stallion, trying to kick out of my grasp. She's cursing, screaming, and falling all over the place, and she is one hundred percent at my mercy. Suddenly, she changes her tactics and manages to work her way into my lap. Shit, thank God my dick isn't hard anymore, but hell, if she keeps twisting around in my lap…

I'm only really ticklish under my arms. She jams her fingers into my armpits, and I lock my arms tight to my sides. Her hands might be there, but there's no way she can move them.

She tilts her head at me. "Relax, Will."

I shake my head. "Nope, you're untrustworthy."

She wiggles in my lap some more, and I'm fucked. I need to get her off of me before she notices the stiffy I'm getting. I stand, hauling her up with me and drop her back on her side of the couch. When I sit, I pull the blanket across me to help camouflage my wood. She gives me a weird look, and I look away.

"Are you cold?" she asks.

I don't say anything and watch as she stretches back out across the sofa, trying to make sure I can't see up her shorts again. I hold back a grin when I spy a flash of cheek again.

She must have seen it, though. "What?" She asks. "You took away my blanket."

I wad up the blanket and throw it at her face and adjust so she won't notice.

"You suck."

I grin.

When I get back to my house, I have a raging case of blue balls. That girl got me hard at least three times today. It's late. My mom's already in bed, and my dad's out of town on business. I hop into the shower. My hands go straight for my cock. I lean back against the side wall and stroke myself. I picture her, earlier that day, laid out underneath me in the grass. I imagine what it would feel like to touch her, and I think about that hint of ass I saw before.

It doesn't take me long to get close. I have this picture in my head, this dream. It does it for me every time. I see myself lying on my back, on a bed, and her naked, crawling toward me. My whole body tenses as I cum. Afterward, I feel the tension drain from me. I get out of the shower and towel off before collapsing into bed.

I'm almost asleep when a thought wakes me up. She has a fucking date with Kyle Nelson.

I pull up in front of Sarah's house. I'm getting out to go ring her bell when she comes running out and then turns around and runs back in. I laugh and sit back down. She is *always* forgetting shit. I'm used to it by now. She comes out again, and I get a good look at her. Damn, she looks amazing. She's wearing a dress. She almost never wears dresses. Christ, and this one's short too. I watch her legs as she walks over to my car.

She hesitates before sliding in. "Won't Jessica be pissed that you picked me up first?"

Screw her, I think as I shrug. After a couple of minutes, I ask her if her dress is new.

When she shakes her head, I mumble, "I've never seen you wear it."

She laughs. "Because I wear dresses all the time."

It takes everything I have not to reach out and touch her. I take a deep breath. "You look nice."

She smirks at me. "For a tomboy, right?"

I'm at a red light. I take my time looking at her, letting her know I'm looking at her. "You don't look like a tom boy tonight, Miller Lite."

We drive in silence the rest of the way to Jessica's house. She fiddles with the hem of her dress while I try and keep my eyes on the road and not her thighs. She gets out and hops in back when I get to Jessica's house. I don't even bother going to the door, I just stay in her driveway and honk. Once she's in the car, she says something to Sarah, but I'm already tuning her out.

I keep sneaking glances at Sarah in the rearview. One time, she sticks her tongue out at me, and I have to bite back a smile. I tense up when we get to

Kyle's house. It's really pissing me off that he's Sarah's date and not me.

When he gets in, he tells her she looks pretty. Why didn't I tell her she looked pretty? She smiles shyly at him. Fuck. It'll kill me if she actually likes him. I'm ready to deck him when we get to the Multiplex. In line for the tickets, he stands way too close to her.

I glance back at him. Did he just fucking smell her? I buy her ticket even though I know it'll piss him off. He looks annoyed but tries to play it off, asking Sarah about her ring.

She looks at me. "I love it, wear it every day."

Hell yeah. I can't help it, I grin. I'm too busy feeling all pumped up over Sarah loving the ring I got her that I miss Kyle getting her candy and an Icee. I really am starting to hate him. I get an extra large popcorn to share with her. Jessica doesn't like popcorn, and Kyle can play in traffic if he thinks he's getting any. Plus, if we're sharing popcorn, she'll have to sit next to me. So we end up sitting Kyle, then Sarah, me, then Jessica. The armrests can move, so I push the one between us up and put the popcorn there.

During the movie our hands bump a few times when we reach for popcorn at the same time. Each time, she looks at me and smiles, and I know I don't care when or how, but someday, someway, Sarah Miller and I are going to be together.

HER

When we finish the popcorn, I tuck the container under my seat and rest my hand between us. I'm crazy, but I have to touch her. I inch my hand over as close as I can get it without being obvious and just barely touch her thigh with my pinkie finger. She has to notice it. I stare at her out of the corner of my eye and rejoice when she doesn't move away from me. Then I notice that fuckwad put his arm around her. I turn and glare at his hand on her shoulder.

She looks at me, sees my expression and moves her leg away from my hand. Well that fucking sucks. I move my hand and rest it on my leg. All I can think about for the rest of the movie is his fucking arm around her. That should be me.

The girls go to the bathroom after the movie. Kyle tries to talk to me in the hallway, but I fake reading upcoming release posters so he'll leave me alone. Sucks, I used to like Kyle before he tried to date Sarah. On the way back to the car, I suggest ice cream. There's this place Sarah and I always go to. I've never brought Jessica there.

Jessica and Kyle check out the menu while I order for Sarah and me. She knocks her hip into mine when I pay. I grin. I hope it pisses Nelson off. We talk with Jim, the clerk, while we wait for them. He asks about college, surprised that we're going to different schools.

Jessica comes up behind me, wrapping her arms around my waist, letting him know she'll take care of me. It kills me when I see Sarah flinch. Nice time to act possessive, Jessica. I go ahead and pay for their ice cream too, and we all walk outside.

They both got cups. I feel a sense of solidarity with Sarah that we always get waffle cones. We just mesh. I finish first and sit quietly while they eat theirs. I glance at Jessica. I've got to break up with her if I'm going to have any shot with Sarah.

Kyle asks if we all want to go hang out at his house. He has a hot tub, and as much as I want to see her in it, there is no way I want him to. I make up some shit about my mom needing me for something, and Sarah says her head hurts. No hot tub for Kyle is all I can think.

I drop him off first, and the asshole has the balls to ask her for her number, and she gives it to him. In her defense he did put her on the spot, asking her in front of us.

Once he's out of the car, Jessica turns back to her. "I told you he likes you."

And then her phone buzzes.

"Oh my gosh, is that from Kyle?" Jessica asks.

When she nods I roll my eyes. Jessica doesn't stop gushing until we get to her house. When I stop the car, she whines. "Babe. I thought you were going to drop me off last."

I glance back at Sarah. Not a chance. Sarah looks away when Jessica pouts and puts her hand on my thigh. Shit, why does she have to do that in front of her? I fake cough and say I'm coming down

HER

with something. She blows me a kiss and gets out, shaking her ass all the way up the driveway. Half the guys in my class would be all over her, but I just can't wait to be done with her.

I look back at Sarah. "Coming up front?"

She watches Jessica's front door shut. "Are you sure it's okay?"

I almost laugh. "Don't be a dork. Get up here." I pat the passenger seat.

I laugh and call her certifiable after she runs around the car, almost diving into the front seat. On the way back, I change the channel from the crap Jessica put on and start to turn it up before I remember Sarah said her head hurt.

"How's your head."

She looks at her hand and starts spinning her ring. "I kinda lied about my head hurting."

I'm ear to ear grinning. If she liked Kyle, she would have wanted to hang out at his house. "That's cool. I lied about my mom needing me."

"And your cough?"

I just laugh.

I've never broken up with someone before. I don't want to hurt her feelings, but I never should have dated Jessica in the first place. I'll just tell her it's not her, that it's me, and we've grown apart. I park in front of her house and sit in my car to put off going inside.

Something catches my eye from the passenger seat, sort of wedged between the seat and backrest. I lean over and pull it out, smiling when I see what it is. It's a small tin of lip gloss. Sarah's. I can still picture her digging through her bookbag yesterday looking for it.

I go to set it in the cup holder between the front seats but stop. Opening it, I pause to smell it. The melon scent hits me, and I wonder what it would be like to taste Sarah's lips. Guilt comes next. This isn't fair to Jessica. It's not her fault I like someone else. I push the lid on and drop it quickly before I'm tempted to smell it again. Getting out of my car and walking up to Jessica's house, I mentally repeat, 'it's not you, it's me' over and over to myself.

I want this over. I push the doorbell confidently, thinking tops this might take ten minutes. Jessica answers the door with half a smile. She reserves her full smile for when people are watching us.

I follow her into the living room. "Hey, I think we should talk."

She stops in front of the couch, her back to me. "About what?"

She hasn't turned around. I don't want to break up with her when she has her back turned.

HER

"Maybe you should sit down," I say, thinking she would have to look at me that way.

She spins, her eyes flashing. "Maybe I should sit down? William Price, are you trying to break up with me?"

Oh shit. My pause and failure to immediately tell her no sets her off.

"You've got to be kidding me."

I take a step back. "It's not you; it's me."

She shakes her head, crossing her arms over her chest. "Have you been cheating on me with Sarah?"

Does mentally count? "What? No, I haven't cheated on you."

"You don't have to do this, Will. We're perfect together." She takes a step towards me.

I turn my head and look down. "That's the thing. We both know we're not. I am so sorry if I hurt you, but I just can't do this anymore."

She whirls around and steps back to the couch, slowly sinking down onto it. "She's nothing special."

My eyes snap to hers. "Let's leave Sarah out of this."

"How can I? We both know you're doing this for her."

5

It's been over a week since I broke up with Jessica, and I still haven't told Sarah how I feel about her. It's official. I'm chickenshit when it comes to her. It's the first day of spring break. Annual tradition for our school is to go to the local amusement park. The temperature has been warm enough that this year the waterpark is already open. I wait outside her house and laugh when I watch her run back in for something.

"Got everything, Miller Lite?" I joke as she climbs in.

"Shut up." She punches my arm.

"Someday I'm going to pick you up, and you will have everything you need the first time you come out."

She rolls her eyes and puts on her sunglasses before pulling her hair up into a ponytail.

"Alright, William, whatcha waiting for?"

I stare at her. What am I waiting for? Should I tell her how I feel right now? What if she doesn't feel the same way? I held off for so long just because I didn't think she was interested in dating anyone period. After she agreed to go out with Kyle, I knew it would be a matter of time before other guys started asking her out. The only thing that scares me now is if she doesn't feel the same way, I will lose her as a friend.

As I back out, she asks to open the sunroof. I laugh and nod.

"Are we picking up anyone else?"

I shake my head. "Nope, you're stuck with me. I expect you to be entertaining the whole drive."

She leans her seat back and puts her feet up on the dash. "God, too much pressure. Just put on some music."

"Actually," I reach over, pushing her feet down and open the glove box, pulling out a CD before shutting it. "My dad got me something to practice my Italian."

My mom, dad, and I are going to go to Italy for a month over the summer. My mom's family is originally from Naples, and even though she grew up in the States, she still goes back once a year to visit relatives. I haven't been since the summer of sixth grade. I want to go, but I don't. It'll be my last summer with Sarah before we start college, and it sucks that I'll be away from her for part of it.

The rest of the drive, we repeat common Italian phrases. When we get to the park, we head straight for the Z section of the parking lot. This is where everyone is supposed to be meeting up. When we get out, I can't help but notice Jessica three cars over, standing really close to Kyle Nelson. Like something is clearly up with them so close. Sarah

HER

looks up at me. I can give a crap about Jessica. I just don't want her to be a bitch to Sarah.

"So rides first or waterpark?" Sarah asks.

I put my arm around her shoulders as we walk over to everyone. "Rides first, always rides first."

Jessica sees us and rolls her eyes. God, why did I ever date her? We wait for some more of our classmates to show before descending on the park. Sarah and I have season passes so we don't have to wait in line with everyone else. It was my birthday present to her this year, that and funnel cake. Funnel cake is her favorite and definitely on the agenda for today.

Before meeting me, Sarah had never gone on a roller coaster. She sometimes gets motion sickness, doesn't stop me from dragging her on every ride, and miraculously, she's never thrown up. Since school is out, the lines are bad. There seem to be some other schools meeting up here today too.

We're waiting in line for one roller coaster. When the line moves, I grab her hand, pulling her forward to catch up. When we catch up, though, I don't let go, just keep holding her hand. I tug her towards the queue for the first car. I love the way her hand feels in mine. I'm not letting go.

"So after this one want to grab some funnel cake?" I ask, leaning down.

She isn't short, but I still have at least six inches on her. "Hells yeah."

I grin, pulling on her ponytail.

"So you two finally hook up?"

We both turn at the sound. It's Jessica and Kyle. She stands, twirling a piece of her blonde hair as Kyle fidgets next to her, his hand hesitating before resting on her shoulder

I let go of her hand. "Shut up, Jessica."

"What, you can't tell she's hot for you?" she goes on.

I look down at Sarah. "Just leave her alone, Jessica. You know we're just friends."

Why did I say that? Why didn't I just say I would be lucky to have Sarah like me?

The cars pull up, and we step into the first car. As it slowly makes its way up the first drop, I turn to her. "She's such a bitch. You okay?"

She nods, not saying anything.

We're almost at the top. I turn my head to face her. "Come on. Talk to me."

"I'm good." She's lying.

After the ride ends I stop and buy the picture of us from the ride booth. I have an album of them at home. This one isn't our best. I look annoyed, and Sarah looks sad. She runs off to the bathroom. Meanwhile, I think of a way to cheer her up.

When she walks up, I drape my arm around her shoulder and point to the funnel cake stand. "My treat."

"Twist my arm."

She still seems down. When she asks if we should head to the waterpark, I have another idea of a way to cheer her up. "When was the last time we rode bumper cars?"

She laughs. "Like a billion years ago."

She shivers when I put my arm around her as we walk. I look down at her and lick my lips.

There isn't a line when we get there. The attendant glances around to see if anyone else is coming before he waves us on.

"I'm coming for you," I tease, pulling the strap over my head.

"You can't catch me," she shouts back.

She shivers again, even though it's hot out.

The music turns on as the cars come alive. She takes off only to back track and turn away when I go the opposite direction. With all of the empty cars on the track, she has to fight her way through them as I barrel towards her. She screams but manages to get away. She looks back at me, and I wink. That girl. I come right up behind her, and she cuts over to the right, turning the opposite direction before I can get her.

Now she's behind me. I grimace as I try to get away from her, but it's no use. She laughs loudly as she bumps me into the tires lined up the middle of the track. I hang my head in shame before whipping around to come after her again. This time, she has nowhere to run and we're nose to nose while I bump my car into hers. We're both grinning as the music and cars turn off.

"Waterpark?" I ask as we walk out.

"Waterpark!"

We're at a bank of lockers.

My mouth drops when she takes off her tank top. "You're wearing a bikini."

She crosses her arms over her chest, which only pushes her breasts up.

"I've just never seen you in one before," I continue, unable to take my eyes off of her.

"Stop looking at me," she snaps.

"Sorry." I look away, hating every guy here who might be looking at her right now.

I hold my hand out for her tank top. She hands me her shorts too, and I sneak a peek at her while I take off my shirt. She looks incredible.

I'm looking down when I hear something that sounds like a smack. "Who knew Miller had a nice rack?" Josh Jamison jokes behind us.

"JJ, touch my ass again, and I'll chop off your hand," Sarah says.

The fuck? I stand up. "He touched your ass?" I look at her before getting in JJ's face. "You touched her ass?"

"Chill, man" he says, taking a step back.

Nobody should get to touch her but me. "That's not cool. Say you're sorry."

"What?" JJ and Sarah both say at the same time.

I take another step towards him, and JJ shrugs. "Ah, sorry, Sarah. I was only joking."

"Don't do it again," she says, shaking her finger at him.

He smiles but frowns when he looks back at me "I'll see you guys later," he says, taking off.

I can't believe some guy just smacked her ass while she's standing right next to me. He never would have done that if we were together. Are guys going to be hitting on her all day?

My back is to her. She tugs on my arm. "Will?" When I don't say anything, "William."

I turn around and look at her. I'm still annoyed he touched her. "I think I like you better in a one piece."

"What the hell does that mean?" She picks up her bag and shoves it into the locker.

"You just look really nice." I manage before growling. "I'm seriously thinking about kicking his ass."

"Oh." She bumps her hip against mine "It's just JJ. He's harmless."

"He still shouldn't be touching you."

She groans and rolls her eyes.

I shrug, wishing I could touch her. "Just saying."

"Whatever. Slides, wave pool, or lazy river?"

I know she likes the lazy river the best. "It was a long," I dip my head, "walk over here."

She grins, then grabs my arm and pulls me over to the lazy river. I don't want her floating away from me so I rest my foot on her tube so she's stuck with me. We talk about Italy, and when we're passing under a small footbridge, I see some guys from our school.

"Hey, Will. Who's that girl?"

How do they not recognize her? She lowers her glasses.

"Oh shit! That's Sarah Miller."

She blushes and pushes her sunglasses back up. I just wish they'd stop looking at her.

"Will, you hittin' that?"

That's it. I take my foot off of her raft and grab her hand so they can see. I look back at them like what?

"Damn. Go Price is right man."

She tugs her hand out of mine. "You just made them all think we're together."

She says it like it's a bad thing. I drop my head back so the top of it gets wet before sitting back up and looking at her "I'm just trying to look out for you."

"I don't think I need to be looked after," she grumbles.

She sounds annoyed. "God, I wish you wore a one piece." I look over at her. "When did you even buy that?"

Her mouth drops, and she just stares at me. "Well?"

When she sniffles, I get that I just hurt her feelings. "I thought you said I looked nice before."

Fuck it. I flip over on to my stomach and dog paddle over to her. When I get to her, I rest my chin on the side of her raft and look up at her. Time to grow some balls, Will. I lower my shades so she can see my eyes. "You don't look nice. You look fucking hot."

When she doesn't say anything back, I push off of her tube and float away. What the fuck did I just do? I just ruined our friendship. Neither of us say anything when we make our way from the lazy river and we go further into the park to the water slides.

I want to keep her by my side, so I grab her hand and pull her to the line for the tandem slide. I sit in the tube first, and she hesitates before sitting in front of me, between my legs, her back to my chest. This would be a very bad time to get a hard on.

I wrap my arms around her waist. She gently lays her hands on my arms, raising them when I unwrap my arms from her waist. She just isn't close enough. I put my hands on her shoulders as I pull her towards me so that she's lying against me before circling her waist with my arms again.

She feels stiff. I whisper in her ear. "Relax."

She leans her head back against me, turning her face so I can feel her breath on my neck.

All at once, we're flying after the attendant uses his foot to propel our tube down the slide. My grip on her tightens as I lean forward, my cheek pressing against hers. We crash into the water a tangle of arms and legs.

When she stands and turns her back to me, I suck in a breath and go to stand behind her, my body pressed against her. She looks back at me, her mouth falling open when I reach down to fix the bottom of her bikini. She blushes. At some point during our slide, her suit shifted. I look down at her, and she mouths 'thank you,' my hands still on her. This is it. I'm going to kiss her. I lean forward and watch as she wets her lips.

"Get you some, Price!"

I close my eyes, ready to deck whoever interrupted us. I pause then look over. Kyle and Jessica are standing to the side of us.

She glares at me. "Never knew you had a thing for SPT, Will."

Sarah stiffens and pulls away. Fuck. Jessica is such a fucking bitch. I glare back at Jessica, who just smirks, before chasing after Sarah. Once I catch up to her, I drape my arm around her shoulders as we make our way to our towels. Grabbing hers, I wrap it around her.

I look back at Jessica, who is still watching us as I tug on her towel, pulling her towards me and gently kissing her forehead. She looks up at me, trying to blink away threatening tears.

"You are not plain. You are beautiful, Sarah, inside and out. She only says those things because she's a jealous cunt." I wish she could see herself the way I do.

HER

She gives me a half smile, and we walk over to the wave pool. Usually I grab a board and she watches me while I try not fall off it. This time, after we lay out our towels, I pull her in with me. She bumps my hip with hers and tilts her head over to where they keep the boards stacked. I shake my head and pull her in deeper. This is the perfect time to tell her how I feel about her.

Instead, I chicken out again and pick her up and toss her into a wave. She looks so cute when she comes up sputtering. She crinkles her nose and comes after me. I just grab her and pull her under. She's pressed up against me, and she looks really hot in that bikini. I can only handle so much. The waves push her body against me, and I get hard. I'm pretty sure she feels it too. I drop my arms, and we both tread water for a couple minutes.

She isn't looking at me. Shit. This is bad. I gnaw on the side of my lip trying to think of a way to play it off. Ignoring it seems to be the only option. I grab her hand, and she follows me back to our towels. We both lie face down, facing each other. She looks tired, and I smile at her as I watch her eyes close.

I start dozing, but my eyes snap open and I lift my head when I hear, "What the hell, JJ? You're dripping on me."

JJ is standing over her, dripping water on her.

"Seriously, dude. Back off." I'm already standing.

"Chill out, Will. Hey, Sarah. Do you want to come in with me?"

She starts to say something, but I cut her off. "She's good."

She glares at me before turning over and looking up at JJ. "I'd love to."

I grumble and get up to follow them. No more pussyfooting around. I catch up to them once they're only a couple steps in. I grab her from behind and swing her around and up onto my shoulder. I am telling her how I feel about her before someone else hits on her.

"I can walk, you know," she grumbles.

I lower her slowly, sliding her down my body. Her eyes are wide, and I hesitate, chewing on the corner of my bottom lip.

"What the hell was that, Will?"

I shrug, my hands still on her waist. She puts her hands on my chest to push me away; I only hold on tighter.

Exhaling, I close my eyes and lean down to rest my forehead on hers "Why did you have to wear that today?"

"You suck, Will." My eyes pop open. "I'm way more covered up than most of the girls in our class, and I don't see you giving them any grief."

"I just don't like the way other guys are looking at you." I hate how jealous I sound even though I mean it.

Her arms relax, but she doesn't remove her hands. "Why?"

This is it. I turn my head, my breath tickling her ear. "Maybe I want you all for myself."

Her mouth drops open. I lift my head and study her expression. She hasn't freaked out. I slowly lower my lips to hers. I've never been so scared as I barely dust my lips across hers before pressing more firmly.

She jerks back. "Will, what are you doing?"

Her pulling away freaks me out. "I'm trying to kiss you."

She smacks my arm.

"Remember when I told you I like someone else?"

She nods. All I want to do is kiss her again.

"I was talking about you," I admit, relief washing over me.

"Me?" She doesn't believe me.

I roll my eyes and pull her back into my arms.

She pushes me away "But why?"

I put my hands on her shoulders and drop my head down in front of hers. "I've liked you for a long time but just figured you weren't interested in dating anyone, until you agreed to go out with Kyle."

She shakes her head. I can't believe she still doesn't believe me. "Be serious."

I don't say anything. I just drop my lips to hers again. This kiss is to convince her. She braces her hands on my arms and presses herself against me. I keep one arm coiled around her waist and move the other one up to the back of her neck pulling her face closer to mine. She moans, and I use it as an invitation to slip my tongue into her mouth.

Kissing her is better than any fantasy I have ever had. There is no way I could have imagined her soft lips or how turned on I could get from just the taste of her tongue. Her eyes stay closed, and I kiss my way across her cheek to her ear, where I whisper that I've wanted to do that for so long. My mouth moves down to her neck.

"Will, stop."

"What?" I'm nibbling on her earlobe.

"People are watching." She tries to step back.

My arm tightens around her again. "Fuck them."

She laughs. "Will."

I pull back, putting my hands on either side of her face and lock eyes with her. "Seriously, Sarah. Fuck them." I lean back down, giving her a sweet kiss before wrapping my arms around her waist.

"Will?"

"Um hmm." I'm running my nose down the side of her ear. I can just barely smell her apple shampoo. Makes me want to taste her.

"What does this mean?"

"You're mine."

She snorts. "I'm yours?"

"Yep, all mine." I grin, thinking of how fun it will be to make her mine in every way I can.

6

From the park we head home, stopping to get ice cream on the way. After the most perfect afternoon of my life, we get caught napping poolside by my mom. I had talked Sarah into a private swim in my pool. I had her all to myself and didn't have to worry about anyone looking at her. I'd never been so turned on. I had to make myself stop touching her.

I didn't want to scare her or move too fast. She fell asleep in my arms. It would have been amazing to wake up with her there if my mom hadn't caught us. My mom wanted to talk, whatever that meant. I just didn't want this day with Sarah to end.

She opens the front door, and I pull her upstairs to her bedroom, shutting the door behind me. She kicks off her flip flops and lies on her bed. She is so beautiful, and my girlfriend. I've been waiting for this forever. Click. I snap a picture of her when she isn't looking. I set my camera back in its case then step out of my shoes before I go to stretch out next to her. I'm on my side, facing her.

My hand moves up to her face to brush some hair behind her ear. Her smile lights up her whole face. We move closer together until she puts her hands on either side of my face. I snake my arm around her waist. We kiss, and I pull her even closer as my tongue dips into her mouth. We're like this when Brian opens her bedroom door.

We spring apart as Brian mutters, "You have got to be fucking kidding me."

I look up at him, and when I see the look in his eyes, I quickly look back down.

"Ahhh" is all Sarah can come up with.

"How long has this been going on?" He gestures between the two of us.

I reach out to take her hand. "Not long."

"And you're already making out like that on her bed? Wait, don't you have a girlfriend?" Brian's going to kick my ass.

"They broke up."

"And my little sister is your rebound?"

Hell no. I shake my head. "She's not a rebound. I broke up with Jessica for her."

I look at her, and she smiles. Her whole face lights up, and I forget Brian for a moment while I just look at her.

"Sarah, go to my room. I want to talk to Will alone." Brian pops his knuckles.

Oh shit. Now I just watch his hands. "What? No way. Anything you want to say to Will you can say in front of me."

I squeeze her hand and lie. "It's okay, Sarah."

Brian motions towards his room with his head.

"Fine," she grumbles, giving my hand a squeeze one more time before she lets go.

Brian closes the door behind her and leans against it. "What are your intentions with my baby sister?"

I go to stand, but he motions for me to stay seated. "I would never hurt her," I say with conviction.

He rubs his jaw. "You're lucky I believe you, but this." He motions to the bed. "Is too soon."

I nod, wondering if this means he isn't going to kick my ass.

"What's your new favorite word, Will?"

Huh? My confusion must read across my face because he answers for me. "Slow. Slow is your new fucking favorite word. Got me?" He pushes off against the door, towering over me.

"Yes," I say quickly.

I really don't want to get my ass kicked. It would put a damper on it being the best day of my life. I go home to face the music with my mom. Our chat is surreal. She also wants to know what my intentions are with Sarah. She amazes me by asking why I'm not still with Jessica and goes on to say what a nice girl Jessica is.

I hadn't even known she noticed I dated her, let alone paid enough attention to have an opinion on whom I dated at all. She's disappointed when I make it clear I have no plans on ending things with Sarah, period.

"So what color is your dress?" I've never been into school dances, but I'm excited about prom.

She closes her locker. "Not telling you."

I smile and grab her hand. "I just need to know what color corsage to get you."

"Oh, I thought you—never mind. It's black."

Is the flower supposed to match the dress? "Do they have black flowers?"

She giggles. "Black goes with anything, silly. We can pick whatever color we want."

"So what color corsage do you want?"

She pauses, looking at me. "I don't know, white or red. What do you think?"

I slip her backpack down her arm and toss it into the backseat before kissing her "Anything you want," I whisper in her ear as I kiss her neck.

"I want you."

Did she just say that? I lift my head and stare into her eyes. "I'm sorry. I missed that."

She blushes but keeps her eyes on mine. "I want you."

"You got me, Miller Lite."

"Will," she groans.

"What?" I ask innocently, trying not to think of how dead I would be if Brian found out.

We turn our heads when someone shouts across the parking for us get a room. I kiss her again and reach behind her to open the door for her. When we're both in my car, I turn and ask if she's okay.

She looks down and starts to spin her ring. "Do you want to, you know, have sex with me?"

I gulp. "Of course, but I don't want you to feel rushed."

"I don't," she lifts her eyes to mine, "want to wait."

She says it again. "I don't want to wait."

I grab her neck and pull her mouth to mine, my fingers threaded through her hair. A tap on the driver's side window brings us back to earth. Our school's track coach motions for us to hit the road. I nod, catching my breath and shifting in my seat before I start the car.

Once we're on the main road going towards her house, I speak. "Are you sure?" As much as I want her to, I just don't want her to feel pressured.

"I love you," she answers.

I take her hand and kiss her knuckles while I drive, feeling like the luckiest guy on the planet. "I love you so much, Sarah Miller. So much."

Slow has been my favorite word for the last two months. I've been letting her set the pace. I would be willing to wait forever for her. Yesterday, she told me she wanted to have sex with me and then that she loved me. Part of me wanted to do it right then and there or when we were messing around on her couch afterward, but I can't.

I don't want her first time to be like that. I want it to be something she'll never forget. I'm thinking prom night. Until then, I want her to get used to me touching her without being shy or nervous.

I've been dreaming about what I'll do to her all day. From the moment I got to her house this morning and saw she wore a dress like I asked. Yesterday was unreal. I've never seen anything as sexy as her face when I was touching her. Today, if she's okay with it, I want to try something different. I'm getting turned on just thinking about it. When I turn the corner and see her waiting for me by my locker I have to tell myself to calm down.

I pull her in for a kiss. She leans into me, and it's like she was built to fit me. She breaks our kiss first, her eyes glancing nervously around to see if anyone saw us. She's beautiful.

I let my hand drift down her back until they land on her waist before dropping a kiss on her forehead. She steps back and tilts her head toward my locker. Oh, right, books. I shrug my bookbag off and open my locker, dumping what I don't need. Once I'm all set, I drape my arm across her shoulders, and we walk out to the parking lot. When we get to my car, I kiss her again and open her door.

HER

Once I'm in, before I've even started my car, I reach out and skim the edge of her dress with my fingers. "I like your dress."

She shivers, and it makes me feel invincible. By some miracle, we make it to her house in one piece.

"Should we go to your room?" I ask, not really wanting to do what I want to do to her in the den.

Her eyes widen, and she nods. We drop our bags by the door, and I pull her into my arms. I love that she's smaller than me, that I have to lean over to kiss her while she stands on her toes. I can't get enough of her. I have every intention of taking it slow with her. Her hair is down today. My hands are at the back of her neck; my fingers sink into her hair. I pull back, breaking our kiss and watch as her eyes focus on mine.

"Upstairs." I lean in to whisper in her ear.

She yelps and wraps her arms around my neck as I sweep my arm under her and carry her up the stairs. Her eyes stay on mine each step. I use my foot to kick the door closed behind us once we're in her room. I watch her eyes dart around and bet she's wondering if it's messy or if she should have made her bed.

I walk over to her bed and gently set her down. She reaches over to slip off her shoes. I'm nervous about taking mine off in case we need to hurry downstairs if her mom gets home early. I finally decide to take them off and crawl up next to her.

She's on her back, her fingers linked on her chest, my very own Snow White. I lean over her and kiss her. Her hands move up to my hair. I can tell she's getting turned on when she flexes her fingers against my head. I lower myself onto my side, and she turns to face me. I love the feeling of being over her, but I can either hold myself up or touch her, and I'm dying to get my hands on her.

She's wearing a button up sweater over her dress. There is nothing hotter than her eyes on mine as I unbutton it. I push one side over her shoulder, and she sits up to take it all the way off. Her dress is sleeveless, and when she lies back down, I lightly drag my fingertips down her arm and watch goosebumps form.

Learning all of the ways her body will react to me is my newest obsession. Every day I can discover some new way to want her. That thought leads me to her breasts. She slips her arms through both of the straps of her dress and her bra. I kiss her as my hand palms her over her clothes.

With my lips on hers, I tug the material covering it down. When my hand cups bare skin, I'm beyond turned on. Her arm reaches down to my waist to pull my body closer to hers. She doesn't shy away from my hard on. She presses her hips against mine and swivels them in a way that makes me want her so bad.

I lift my head to check the time on her alarm clock. It's hard to stop kissing her when I look back down at her. Her eyes flutter open, and her lips are parted. I can't ignore them, but I still have plans for her. I dust my lips across hers as I move lower. I kiss my way down her neck, nipping along the way. When my lips hit the sensitive skin around her breasts, her body bucks against mine.

God, she turns me on. I take a deep breath before I lower my hand to her hip as I explore her further. She murmurs things softly. I have to make myself listen over the sound of blood pounded in my ears. "Oh, Will. Oh, oh, whoa, yes."

And when she sucks in her breath, I know I'm doing something right. My hand moves from her hip to the hem of her dress. I lift my lips from her breast to watch her eyes as I pull the material higher up her leg. She shivers again. Shit. Something about watching her tremble gets me even more worked up. I slowly kiss my way down her stomach, over the top of her dress. I keep my eyes on hers just in case she wants me to stop. It would be hard, but I won't push her.

Her dress is pulled up far enough for me to kiss the tops of her thighs. Each kiss, I pause to look up at her. She's wearing simple pink cotton underwear. I hear her gasp when I kiss the seam. I lift my head. "Is this okay?"

She doesn't say anything, just gives me a small nod. My eyes lock on her as I reach up to ease her underwear down. She lifts her hips just a breath, just enough for me to know she trusts me. This, what I'm about to do, is a first for me too. I stare at her, right in front of me. She is so fucking beautiful. I'm pretty sure I was doing something right yesterday so I start touching her first with just my hands. She's moaning. Holy shit, that's hot. I drop my lips to her and pull back when her hips buck.

"Easy, Miller Lite." I laugh.

Her hands cover her face. I crawl up her to push them away and kiss her. I don't want her to be shy or embarrassed. She's a fucking dream come true.

"Do you want me to stop?" Please say no, please say no.

I chew on the inside of my lip, waiting for her to reply, then kiss her again when she shakes her head and quietly says. "Don't stop."

That's all I need. I hear her giggle as I ease myself back down her body. Her parents might be home any minute, and I want to make this good for her. With my fingers and my lips, I touch and kiss every inch of her. Stopping and staying wherever it is that makes her start moving underneath me.

I'm hard as a rock, but all I can focus on is her, her sounds, her taste, how soft she is, how wet I've made her. Her fingers are in my hair, and I'm surprised by how sexy it is to feel her push my head down to her. I love the effect I have on her body. I don't stop; I feel like whatever I am doing is right, is what she needs.

HER

I smile against her when she calls out my name. I'm also scared shitless because that was fucking loud. I'm not stopping, though, not until she's shaking like a leaf and says 'ohmygod' at least six more times.

Only once I'm sure she's done, I lift my head. Her head is thrown back, her chest rising and falling as she struggles to catch her breath. I fix the skirt of her dress so it covers her again.

She lifts her head. "Whoa."

The look in her eyes and how I made her shake is what I plan to picture as I jerk off in the shower tonight. That was exactly what I was hoping for. I look at her clock again and groan. I wish we had more time. She sits up and fixes the top of her dress. I love the way she blushes when I pass her underwear to her.

She slips them on and her shoes before we head back downstairs. I grab our bags and head straight for the den while she goes to the kitchen to get us a snack. I pull books from both bags out and spread them across the coffee table so it looks like we've been doing our homework before flipping on the TV.

Not even five minutes later, her mom walks in. Shit, that was close.

Damn, she's gorgeous. "You are so beautiful" I'm nervous as I slip the corsage onto her wrist.

She looks smoking in her dress. Shit. I can't wait to take it off of her. She moves, and I gulp when I see how far the slit goes. God I love her legs. I can't take my eyes off her as she pins the matching flower thing to my jacket. Her mom goes nuts with the pictures, even getting action shots of us getting into the car. It sucks because if she had stayed in the house I could have Sarah pressed against this car right now.

I just want to kiss her, but the way I want to kiss would not go over well in front of her mom. Brian's course load has him so busy he's only been coming home every other weekend. There is no way Sarah and I could get away what we have been doing if he was around.

Every red light on the way, I kiss her. When she bites my lower lip, it takes the car behind us honking for me to willingly leave her lips. Prom is being held in the ballroom of the community center. After I'm parked, she uses her thumb to wipe lipstick off my lips and reaches into her purse to put some more on. First goal of the night, see how fast I can kiss it all off again.

After we walk in we have our pictures taken again under an arch made out of balloons. A bunch of kids from our class are going to an after party at Bravo's house. We're not. I got us a hotel room.

HER

The people not going to Bravo's are going to a hotel near the community center.

Sarah wanted to get a room so I got one further out. I'm hoping it'll be quiet, romantic. I'm ready to go now. I made prom court, though, so Sarah wants me to stay for the announcement.

When it's finally time, I give her a kiss before I join the rest of the court on stage. Once I'm up there, I find Sarah in the crowd and blow her a kiss. I can see her blush from here. They announce the girls first. Great. Jessica. If I had any desire to be Prom King before, it's gone now.

When they call my name, I act happy, but I don't really feel it until I watch Sarah give me a wolf whistle. That girl. The music starts, and I frown but offer Jessica my arm. I can dance one song with her. As soon as we're done, though, Sarah and I are out of here.

I put my hand up, waltz style, but she just wraps her arms around my neck. Awkward. I try to keep as much distance between us as I can, but she keeps stepping closer. I glance down at her, and she licks her lips. Really? When I feel her fingers move into my hair, I jerk my head to the side.

Fuck this. I put my hands on her forearms and pull her arms down from my neck before turning and leaving her there in the middle of the dance floor. Yes, I may have embarrassed her, but there is no way I'm going to let her disrespect my relationship with Sarah in front of our class. Sarah's looking the other way when I walk up and jumps when I wrap my arm around her waist.

I love it when she looks surprised. "What are you doing?"

That right there. She doesn't want me to miss out on anything. She would probably willingly stand there and watch Jessica try and grope me as long as it meant I was happy. I'm still waiting for her to figure out making her smile is the only thing that makes me happy right now. I pull her out onto the dance floor, doing my best to ignore Jessica.

The dance floor fills up quickly. She looks up at me, and there it is. That smile I would do anything for. I drop my lips to hers. When the song is over, we leave. She talks me into walking out first. She's paranoid people will think we're going to go have sex if we walk out together.

But it's what she wants, so I walk out before her and wait for her by my car. It's warm out and a clear night. The parking lot has no shortage of lampposts and moths and other flying insects swirl around the glow of each. The real beauty of the night is walking towards me. You always hear people talking about love in songs or movies. I never really believed it was as big of a deal as everyone made it out to be.

I was wrong, this girl owns my soul, and I'm the luckiest guy alive because I get to make it my mission in life to make her happy.

HER

She pauses, a subtle hesitation. "We don't have to do anything. I'd be happy to just fall asleep with you in my arms." As much as I want her, I mean it. I would wait a hundred years if she asks me to.

"I know."

I open her door for her.

Once I'm in the car, I turn towards her. "I mean it. We can just kiss and stuff if you want."

"Will, I'm nervous, but I want to, so let's go."

I had checked in earlier and got the room all set up. I want tonight to be perfect for her.

"Are you sure about this?"

She blushes. "Stop asking. I'm sure."

I love her. I slide the key card into the door and open it for her. She doesn't know I decorated it and covers her mouth as she takes it all in. I walk around the room and light candles while she looks around before setting up my iPod.

"I made a playlist I thought you might like."

The first song that comes on is "You're Beautiful." We're across the room from each other. I pull off my jacket and set it down as she walks towards me. I meet her halfway.

"Do you like it?" I ask nervously, hoping she does.

"I love it. Thank you."

"I want it to be perfect for you."

"As long as I'm with you, it will be."

I pull her closer, kissing her forehead. "I love you so much."

"I know. I love you too, so, so much."

She turns in my arms. "Can you unzip me?"

My hands shake as I slowly lower her zipper. I wet my lips as I stare at her bare back. When I drag my fingertips and lean down to kiss her shoulder, she shivers. There's a strap that goes around her neck. I'm not sure how to undo it so I take a step back. She lifts the strap up over her head and holds the front of her dress to her. I gulp and look into her eyes. My mouth drops as her dress falls to the floor.

She covers herself, and I close the space between us. She reaches up to take off my tie, then I help her unbutton my shirt. I tug it and my undershirt off as she reaches for my pants. We're both undressed and on the bed before the next song comes on.

We lay there, facing each other. We've never been all the way naked, both of us, either us, together before. This is the first time I'm actually seeing all of her and she's seeing all of me.

"Can I touch you?"

"Huh?" I gulp. "Sure," I say, dying to have her stroke me.

I turn onto my back and put my hands behind my head. I watch her nervously. She trails her fingers up my cock, a gentle stroke. "Is that okay?"

I can't talk. I just nod. God, then she grasps me, her fingers wrapping around me. My hips pitch, and I groan.

"It's okay. That felt really good."

She giggles. "God, I thought I hurt you."

If she keeps touching me, this might be all over before we even get started. I stop her, turning back onto my side and pulling her back to me.

"I'm nervous I won't be good at it."

I take her face in my hands, lifting it until she will look at me. "Impossible."

"Will it be messy?"

What? Sometimes she completely catches me off guard. I laugh, dropping my hands. "Why would it be messy?"

She covers her face. "Because I've never done it."

I can't help it. I grin.

"What?" She laughs.

"You're cute." I lick my lips before crushing them to hers.

We blur into a mesh of arms and legs. I sink into her, but it feels like she's crawled up inside of me. There isn't a place of her that isn't touching me. I try to go slow. I try as hard as possible to be gentle, but when she starts moving against me, with me, and I can't hold back. I've never done it without a condom before, but since Sarah's on the pill, she said I didn't need one. It feels unreal, warm, wet, tight. She watches me as I fall apart. I'm about to lean down and kiss her when she laughs.

"Something funny?" I'm terrified it didn't feel good for her.

"You just deflowered me."

God, I love her. "Did it hurt?"

"A little at first, but then it felt better." She runs her hands up and down my back. "Was I okay? For you?"

"Okay? Sarah, you crazy beautiful girl. I love you so much. That was the second best moment of my life. The first was when you told me you loved me."

"So that's a good thing, right?" she teases.

She pulls me down, kissing me, pausing only to start laughing again.

She tries to smother her laughs with her hand. "We just did it, Will."

It's infectious. "Why is that funny?"

"I just can't believe it."

"I love you, even when you're a crazy person" I brush my nose against hers.

She stops laughing, now serious. "I've loved you for so long."

I brush some hair off her face, tucking it behind her ear. "How long?"

"Seventh grade."

"You did not."

"Alright, maybe it wasn't *love* love, but I had the biggest crush on you."

"I never knew. I never thought—" I kiss my way down her neck. "I wish I had known."

"Why?"
"We could have gotten together sooner."

7

It's like someone flipped a switch. One minute it was bright, full of light, and Sarah was in my arms. My only mission in life was talking her into going away to school with me. Then bam! Nothing but darkness. I don't know where she went. She's just gone. She was in my arms twenty minutes ago. I'm freaked. I know it. Even Bravo, who is one chill guy, is looking at me like I've lost it. That's just it. I've lost it.

Where is she?

It's not until the hundredth time I've tried her cell that I see it light up inside my car. Fuck. If her phone is here, where is she? I walk out into Bravo's backyard, closer to the water. Could she have fallen in? Shit, what if she's out there struggling right now, and I have no idea? I'm about to get into the water when I hear Bravo call my name as he jogs toward me.

He's out of breath. "Hey man. Some people saw her leave with some girls in a Prius."

"Who saw her? Are they sure it was Sarah? Who drives a Prius?" I turn, searching the faces around me.

"Whoa, man. Breathe. Look, I'm not sure what happened, but she probably just caught a lift home."

I shake my head. "She wouldn't have done that unless something happened." I reach into my pocket for my keys.

"No way, man." Bravo says, grabbing them from me.

"What? I'm fine." I say, reaching for them.

He shakes his head and shoves them into his pocket. "One, you drank tonight. Two, hate to break it to you, but you are not thinking straight at the moment. Go upstairs. Get some sleep and go talk to her in the morning. My nana always said no good decisions are made after midnight."

I want to argue. I want to somehow get my keys from him and take off after her, but Bravo is a good guy so I let him lead me back into the house. Even though it's late, I still call Brian's cell once I'm in my room.

Once he tells me she's home, I relax. He won't let me talk to her, though, which bugs me. Instead, he tells me to come by in the morning.

After I hang up with him, it takes me forever to fall asleep. I just can't figure out why she would leave the way she did. All of her stuff is still in our room. It just isn't like her. She's never done anything like this. Somehow, after what feels like hours, I fall asleep.

HER

When I wake, it takes me a minute to remember where I am, and I realize Sarah isn't with me all over again. I throw all of our stuff together and race downstairs. Bravo is already up and gives me back my keys. Luck is on my side that there aren't any cops out this morning because the speed limit seems optional given what I'm racing back to. Pulling up to Sarah's house, my stomach drops, and I know right away something is wrong.

Mrs. Miller and Brian are both outside, and Brian's cell phone is to his ear. It just keeps ringing.

"Mom," I hear him say as I walk over to them.

Mrs. M sees me and runs over. "Will, do you know where Sarah is? She won't answer her phone."

I look up at Brian, unable to keep the anger from my voice. "I thought you said she was here."

He rubs his hand over his face. "Yes, *was*. Just when we woke up this morning, she was gone, and so is my car. She left a note on her bed saying that she was headed to Jersey. We keep trying to call her but..." He trails off.

I try to wrap my brain around her going to Jersey when I remember I have her phone. "You won't be able to reach her. That's why I called you last night. Her phone was in my car. It must have fallen out of her hands or something."

"Why did she come home early? Did you two have a fight?" Mrs. M asks.

I shake my head. "We didn't fight at all." I point over to my car and show them the dent. "I have no clue why she left. I was all wrapped up dealing with that."

Mrs. M pats me on the shoulder. Sarah ran away? I look up at Brian and hold up my hands.

He watches her walk back into the house before coming over to me. "She was crying in her room last night; I could hear it through her door, but she wouldn't talk to me."

"What the hell? Why didn't you tell me that last night?"

He shakes his head. "I didn't expect her to be gone this morning. She's probably broken down somewhere between here and Jersey, knowing my piece of shit car."

I grab his arm, pulling him toward my car. "Then let's go. We'll just get on 95 and find her and bring her back."

"You think Dad and I didn't already talk about that? Hell, who knows if she was lying in her note. She could be headed anywhere." He starts pacing.

"Your sister isn't a liar," I argue, my words stopping him.

He nods. "I know. That's why my dad is on the phone with my uncle right now."

I blank on his name for a sec. "Chip?"

"Yeah. He's going to let us know if and when she gets there."

This is insane. "So you're going to just sit here and do nothing?" I ask in disbelief.

Mr. M walks out. "Brian, I just got a call from Roger. He found your car."

We both look at him. "Where?"

He frowns. "The train station."

"That means she could have gone anywhere."

I feel lightheaded. I sink to the curb and put my head between my knees. I thought I felt bad last night. This pain is a whole lot worse. It feels like someone reached into my chest, pulled out my heart, and is squeezing it. It hurts to breathe.

I stare, at the dirt and gravel on the ground, trying to make sense of it all. It's like she vanished into thin air. Sarah is my world. Almost every decision I make on a daily basis is done with a consideration of how it would also affect her.

Brian crouches down next to me and pats my back. "Look we'll wait to hear from my uncle."

I shake my head, still looking down. "We don't even know for sure that's where she's going."

"Exactly, so it would be stupid to do anything right now before we find out anything else."

I look up, turning my head to look at him. "I can't just sit here. I have to do something."

He nods. "For now, and I'm not saying this to be harsh, but I think it would be best if you went home. I can call you the second we hear from my uncle."

What do you do when the girl you're in love with runs away?

Do you sit at home and watch a movie? Maybe grab a burger and some fries? I want to go after her with every molecule I'm made of, and it's killing me that I just don't know what direction to go. I rise slowly to my feet, uncertain they'll support my weight. I walk to my car, vaguely hearing Brian promise he'll call me in the background. When I pull into my driveway, I feel the sensation of not even knowing how I got here. I must have been on autopilot the whole drive.

I walk upstairs to my room and torture myself with pictures of her. Where is she? At some point, my mom knocks on the door. I ignore her, committed to my personal hell. I've texted Brian four times asking if they've heard anything and freak out a little more every time he responds that they haven't.

It's nighttime. My stomach growls, but I ignore it, certain anything I'll eat will just come right back up. My dad knocks on my door this time, not waiting for my response and just walking in.

"William, your mother is upset. You've been sulking all day. We have to leave early tomorrow, and she just wants to make sure you're all packed." He glances around my room. His eyes never really coming near me.

Fuck. Italy. I stand. "Dad, Sarah's missing. I can't go to Italy."

His mouth drops, and he finally looks at me. "What do you mean she's missing?"

My mom sticks her head in the doorway. "Who's missing?"

My dad turns back to her. "Will's girlfriend."

"What?" She says, bringing her hand up to cover her mouth.

"What happened?" My dad asks, looking back at me.

I sit up, feeling dizzy when I do and claw at my comforter to keep myself up. "We went to a party at Bravo's last night. Someone dented my car." I ignore their raised brows and keep going, not even caring about my car. "I was exchanging insurance stuff with the girl when Sarah just left with some girls and went home. When I went to her house she was gone. She took a train somewhere. She left a note saying she was going to her uncle's place in New Jersey but…" I just shake my head.

"Sounds like she ran away." My mom sniffs.

"She wouldn't do that. I have to find her, bring her home."

"We leave for Italy in the morning."

I shake my head. "I'm not going."

My dad looks back at my mom. "Maybe we should cancel the trip."

Her eyes widen then fill with tears. "No, please. We have to go. My family. What will they say? Don't say that."

He looks back at me before pulling her gently towards their room. I can hear their voices raise, my mom slipping in some Italian in frustration. After an hour, he comes back to talk to me alone, guilt on full blast. My mom, her feelings, my sister, how could I do this to her. Finally I agree to go, on the condition that the second we get home they won't stop me from looking for Sarah.

He leaves but comes back to bring me some toast and water. I inhale it and go downstairs in search of more food. My mom is on the phone in the kitchen, telling someone we'll see them there. She must be talking to one of our relatives, but usually, she speaks Italian when she does.

I grab an apple and some slim jims and head back to my room. I text Brian again, this time letting him know I'm going to be gone for the next month. My phone doesn't even have an international plan, so I won't be able to get texts or calls once I go. I give him my email address because I'll at least be able to check that.

I make a halfhearted once over of my bags. Thankfully, they were mostly packed a few days ago. The next morning, I feel like I'm on autopilot again. We take a cab to the airport. When we get to our gate I feel like I'm imagining things when I see Jessica and her family waiting there. I stop and look at mom. She ignores my stare and rushes over to hug Mrs. Burton. What the fuck just happened?

HER

Jessica's face breaks into a wide grin when she sees me. "Hey, Will."

"What are you doing here?" I ask, confused.

With total mock innocence, she puts her hand on her chest and widens her eyes. "You didn't know our families were going to Italy together?"

"What?" I turn to my dad.

He shrugs, sitting down with a newspaper.

Jessica reaches for my arm and doesn't even react when I pull away from her. "Mom, why didn't you tell me?"

She smiles at Jessica, who preens under the attention. "I thought you'd be happy your girlfriend was coming."

I stare at her, dumfounded. "Mom. Jessica is not my girlfriend. Sarah is."

My mom rolls her eyes and waves me off, turning back to Mrs. Burton.

I turn, about to walk right out of the airport when Mitch, her little brother, runs over to me. "Hey Will. Isn't this cool? We're going to another country. I'm so happy another boy is going."

Maybe I can use him to shield me from Jessica the whole trip.

I have never felt so good to be home in my life. Yes, Italy was cool. Yes, I was able to take a ton of pictures. Yes, I am happy I got to see some relatives, but ever since Brian emailed me that first week that she did go to her uncle's, I knew that was where I was heading the moment I got home.

I was actually looking forward to being by myself in my car as I drove up there. Jessica barely left me alone the whole time we were away. I don't know how else to make it clear to her I'm not interested. I hope she gives up soon. What's worse is I'm pretty sure my mother was encouraging her.

Our flight didn't get in until tonight late, so I'm leaving in the morning. My mom is pissed, but she should be happy I went to Italy at all. I have no problem falling asleep. It's like my body knows I'm going to see her tomorrow, going to get her and bring her home, and wants to be rested.

I set my alarm for six so I can miss rush hour traffic as I drive out of town. My mom and dad are both still asleep when I leave. It's just me and the road. I look at the empty passenger seat beside me. Since the first day I got this car, she's usually been sitting there.

I can't wait to bring her home. I don't have much of a plan. I understand I probably should. I just figure once she sees me it'll fix whatever it was that made her go away in the first place. She's it for me.

My plan to make it up there in one day is turned to shit by the state of Maryland and some bullshit construction. It's bumper to bumper. I manage to inch my way to an exit and give up for the day. The motel I end up booking a room in looks like something out of a bad seventies horror movie.

I hit the vending machine and have a dinner of a three day expired pack of crumb doughnuts, a strawberry pop tart, and a Mountain Dew. I set the alarm on my phone to make an early start.

It's raining when I get up and doesn't stop until I hit the New Jersey Turnpike. I take it as a sign. The clouds are going away since I'm getting closer to where she is. I glance at my GPS, I'll be at her uncle's place soon.

When I get there, I run up to knock on his door, not expecting there wouldn't be anyone home. I'm hungry so I get back in my car and hit a drive thru so I can eat in my car while I wait for her.

I feel like a creeper sitting here in my car waiting for her. What feels like hours later, a beat up truck pulls into the spot numbered for her uncle's condo. I sit up, groaning as pins and needles shoot up my back from sitting in my car so long. A young guy gets out of the driver side as she gets out from the passenger side.

My pulse starts racing as soon as I see her, my hand on the handle to open my door. It's weird that's she with some guy. They walk toward the bed of the truck. She's smiling at that guy. Sarah is smiling at some guy. My hand falls off the handle and to the edge of my seat. I lean forward, squinting at them. Sarah reaches into the back of the bed and lifts a big stuffed monkey, the kind you win at a fair.

Were they on a date? She throws it at him, laughing. When he catches it, he shakes it towards her, and she laughs even more. I feel like throwing up everything I just ate. I can't believe I'm sitting here, watching my girlfriend on a date.

My vision blurs as I watch her unlock the door, and that guy follow her into the condo, shutting the door behind him.

All I ever wanted in life was to see her smile. I just thought I would be the guy that did it for her. Do I love her enough to step aside if someone else makes her happy? It takes me a full ten minutes to decide to leave. As much as I want an explanation, I'm too scared to hear her tell me she doesn't love me anymore. I'm angry too. At her, at myself. She's moved on.

Something brought her here. It wouldn't be fair to her for me to step in now and to reinsert myself into her life. I'm back on the turnpike before I can actually accept I just saw her with another guy.

I want to figure out a way to erase that image from my mind. Instead, her smiling at someone else seems etched onto my corneas. Until this moment, I have never considered my life without her in it. Even the first day she left, even the whole time I was in Italy, I assumed this was temporary. It isn't temporary. Today might be the last day I'll ever see her. That night might be the last night I ever touched her.

I pull over in a rest area and break down. It feels like a valve has disconnected itself from my heart and is now bleeding from my eyes. I can't see straight. I can barely breathe. My body is physically rejecting the thought of losing her.

A little boy parked in the car next to mine stares at me in abject horror and makes me pull myself together enough to get back on the road. I pull over and take a piss somewhere in Virginia but otherwise drive straight home. It's almost morning by the time I pull into my driveway. I'm starving, but exhaustion has a stronger pull and I just make it to my bed before passing out.

As I wake during that fuzzy time you adjust to being conscious, I haven't yet realized she's gone. I'm seconds into my moment of blissful unawareness when I remember. Then that picture burned on my brain takes away any hope I have. She taunts me from every direction of my room. For the first time in my life, I question the amount of pictures I've taken. She's tucked into every frame. She was my favorite subject.

I feel like I made a mistake in not confronting her. I drove all that way and was too scared to talk to her. What the fuck is wrong with me? My stomach and my need to escape her take me to the kitchen. It's mid afternoon. I haven't eaten anything since lunch yesterday. I eat a bowl of cereal and go back up to my room. I can't throw her pictures away, but I can't look at them either. I end up shoving them into a shoe box and putting them in the far corner of my closet.

What now?

8

Every plan, every dream I had is now altered, but I'm still pulled to her house. After I've showered and changed, I'm on my way there. I need the familiar feeling of her house, even if she's not in it. I text Brian before I leave to make sure it won't be weird. Pulling up to her house, knowing she won't be running out to jump into my car, hits me when I park. I start to get choked up but do my best to shake it when I see Brian open the front door.

I get out and walk over to him. "Hey."

"How are you?"

I shake my head, hoping for a change of subject. "Did you go?"

I nod. My tongue feels swollen and stuck to the roof of my mouth.

He scratches the back of his head. "Do you want to talk about it?"

Why did I even come here? I'm starting to feel like this was a mistake. I don't nod. I don't speak. I stand there incapable of saying I'd love to talk about it, but if I do, I'll probably cry and I don't want to do that in front of him.

After a couple of moments of awkward silence, he invites me in. I fight the impulse to go upstairs and into her room. I miss the way she smells, the way she tastes, the way she fits me, gets me, and the way I thought she loved me. Instead, I stiffly sit on the sofa in her den, with her big brother.

He finally gets up and puts a movie on to find something to fill the silence. When Mrs. M gets home, she pulls me into a hug and makes me promise I won't be a stranger. She asks about Italy, and I'm embarrassed by how little I can tell her. I show her pictures instead, even the ones I don't remember taking.

I excuse myself and leave not long after. Being there is somehow too hard and comforting at the same time. Over the rest of the summer, I find myself there, sitting on her parents' couch, not talking to Brian, a lot. Things get busy at the end of summer as I get ready to go off to college. Life keeps moving that way. I haven't moved on, but I'm a different Will from the one that saw her that day.

I had dreamed of sharing an apartment with her. Of falling sleep with her in my arms every night. Instead, I get a last minute dorm assignment. My roommate, Carl, is an okay guy. He likes to party more than I ever have.

I get sucked into it, the partying, the drinking, the nameless girls. I steer clear of Jessica every time I see her out, but it doesn't stop her from going after Carl as a way to get to me. Waking up with her in my dorm room one time is all it takes to set some ground rules with Carl.

I don't care who he brings home, as long as it isn't her again. At first, he thinks it's because I'm still interested. It doesn't take long to convince him otherwise.

It all still comes back to Sarah.

One night at a party, I sit back and watch as more of a spectator. There is more than one beautiful girl there. It doesn't matter. No matter how hard any of them try to get my attention, it's useless. I feel branded beneath my skin by a girl who left without even saying goodbye. That's when I decide to get a tattoo. I need to be marked on the outside as well.

Carl decides to come along and even makes fun of me for picking a Miller Lite logo, saying it's a bitch beer. He thinks I should get something more manly, like Whiskey or Jåger. This isn't about beer, though. It's about a girl.

Growing up, saying the Pledge of Allegiance, putting your hand over your heart every day. That's where I get it, directly over my left pec. The rest of my freshman year ends up being a blur of too much alcohol, and I just eek out passing grades.

My first day back in Decatur, I find myself sitting on her parents' couch, watching a movie with Brian. He knows, the whole time, that I still need this piece of her even though she is gone. I ask about her, what she's doing, how she is. He always brushes my questions off.

He won't answer them, but he doesn't act annoyed that I still ask. Even not knowing the answers, knowing I'm near someone who does helps me. We hang out a lot that summer and become the friends I'm not sure we could have been if she was around.

Carl wants to room together again our sophomore year, but I end up getting a one-bedroom apartment off campus instead. I just want to keep my head down and focus on school. There are still girls during low points when she seems to haunt me. The relief they offer is brief and unfulfilling.

The summer before my junior year, Brian starts law school and gets his own place. It cramps my still needing to go to her house. Somehow, I think he knows because he makes a point to invite me over whenever he's going over there.

Mrs. M catches on too and reminds me more than once that I'm welcome any time. During school it's easier. I stay there instead of driving home on the weekends and breaks, unless Brian invites me back to his place for something. When he does, half the time I'll just crash at his place. School is a means to an end.

I think I've always known I wanted to be a teacher, especially after that day with Sarah, when we gave our project. There are teachers, like Mrs.

Hall, who recognize when something wrong is happening or a student is being bullied. She didn't make Sarah walk back into our class that day. She let her go to the nurse so she could go home.

Then there are other teachers who are oblivious. I want to be the teacher that notices, the teacher that's there to encourage. Photography has always been important to me. Before I went to school, I was really only goofing off with the pictures I took. I didn't know enough about the light and balance and after editing to ever be serious about it.

I channel everything that's left in me into learning. With practice, it's possible to learn the rules of certain mediums and be able to exist within them. I want to teach basic art. I want to give kids their first structured glimpse into the possibilities of creation. The class I struggle with the most is oil painting. Thank God the state of Georgia sticks to tempora and water-based paints for middle school art.

After I graduate, I buy a place in Brian's complex. I apply all over the place for teaching positions. When I apply to teach at Renfroe, I don't think I have a chance. Given the neighborhood and the schools that feed into it, it's a highly sought after place to teach.

When I get the job there, the first thing I want to do is tell Sarah. I wonder if our separation feels like someone experiencing phantom pain from a lost limb. It's been five years since I've seen her, and my impulse is still to tell her good news. Will that ever go away?

Brian takes me out for drinks to celebrate. That's when I get the call from the hospital. I meet my mom in the emergency room. By the time I get there, my dad has already passed. I know right away my mom isn't going to handle this well.

I take her home that night and sleep in my old room. I handle all of his arrangements. I'm detached throughout the whole process. I was never very close to him. He was always gone. Part of me always hoped that once he retired we would start over, form some type of relationship. I feel the loss of what could have been more than what was.

My mom stops functioning. I try to split my time between my old house and my condo. It's hard with work. I'm in the worst mood the day I meet Christine. She's subbing for a teacher going out on maternity leave, a math teacher. I don't have the best track record with the teacher she's subbing for. She seems to think math supersedes any need for art in a child's life. I'm expecting the same from Christine.

She's not like that at all, and eventually, we become friends. I'm having coffee with her one afternoon when Brian walks past and sees us, sees her. I know this because while I'm still sitting, drinking my coffee, he's already texting me, asking who she is and if I'm on a date. I don't text him back right away, thought it would be rude. I stop by his place when I get home. Once I tell him we're just friends, he asks me to hook him up with her. Christine's a good looking girl, light blonde hair and pale blue eyes. It makes sense she catches his eye.

We talk about ways they can meet. We come up with a plan where she and I can meet for dinner and Brian can just happen to be there. Then once I've introduced them, I'll get a call about some emergency and have to leave.

"Then me, being the nice guy that I am, can offer and stay to keep her company." Brian nods.

"It's genius. It gives you a chance to talk to her one on one, and if you think she's cool, you can ask for her number."

"What if she doesn't want to stay when you have to go?" Brian asks, scratching the back of his head.

"Why wouldn't she stay? Maybe I can ask you to stay. That way, it's like you're doing me a favor."

He nods. "That sounds good."

At school on Monday, I mention this new sushi place to her at lunch. Turns out, she has been wanting to go there. We agree to meet there

Thursday night. We've just ordered our drinks and are looking at the menu when Brian walks up.

"Hey, Will. I thought that was you. Just wanted to say hi."

"Hey, Brian. Christine, this is my friend, Brian. I've known him forever." I look at Brian and try to keep a straight face. "This is Christine. She teaches at Renfroe with me."

She gets red when Brian reaches out to shake her hand. He has his other hand in his pocket, thumb on the call button.

His eyes are still on Christine. "I went to Renfroe. What subject do you teach?" He presses the call button while she answers.

I look at my phone and grimace. "It's my mom. I'm going to take this outside if that's okay."

She nods her head, still looking at Brian. I go outside for a couple minutes, holding my phone to my ear. When I come back inside, I chew on the side of my mouth to keep from grinning when I see them. Brian is now in my seat, and they're both smiling as they talk.

"Hey." I hold my phone up. "That was my mom. She's acting crazy. I think I should go check on her."

"Absolutely. You should go." Christine starts to stand.

I put my hands out. "Please, stay. You wanted to try this place."

"I was going to eat by myself. We can eat together if you'd like."

She starts to shake her head, but I jump in. "Yeah. Eat with Brian, and tomorrow at lunch, tell me if it was any good. Deal?"

She looks at me, then at Brian, then back at me. "Okay. I mean if you're sure it's okay with you?" she asks Brian.

He smiles. "Yeah, and this way you can finish telling me that story you started."

I look at both of them. "So we're good? I'm going to take off."

They both nod, and I leave, heading to my mom's so it feels less like a lie. I stop by the grocery store to pick up a few things for her on the way. She hasn't left the house since my dad passed, wouldn't even go to the funeral. There are bags of trash waiting for me in the foyer. I get the groceries inside before I take them out to the containers on the side of the house. What would she do if I didn't stop by: starve or get buried under garbage?

"Mom!" I call out.

No response. It doesn't surprise me. After Bethany died, she barely spoke to me. I put the groceries away, then head upstairs to look for her. She's sitting on Bethany's bed, brushing the hair of one of her dolls. She's in her robe, and it doesn't even look like she brushed her own hair today. It kills me to see her like this. It's like when Bethany died all over again, only worse.

I lean on the door frame. "Hey, mom."

No response.

"Mom, why don't you put the doll down. Let's go downstairs," I say gently.

Nothing.

Ever since my sister died, I've always felt uncomfortable in her room. I step inside and walk over to my mom, reaching out to touch her shoulder. It takes her a minute before she looks up.

I hold out my hand for her. "Let's go down stairs. I'll make you something to eat."

She sets down the doll and brush and takes my hand. I close the door behind me once we're out of the room. I'm not much of a cook. I make her some soup and a sandwich for myself. I watch her as she eats it. After only finishing a quarter of it, she gets up and leaves.

I follow her. "Mom, are you done with your soup? There's still a lot left."

She nods and heads upstairs to her room, shutting the door behind her. I know what she's doing up there. She's setting my dad's alarm clock for the time he used to get up to go to work. I once read that Queen Victoria had Prince Albert's clothes laid out every morning after he died for forty years. People think it's romantic. It's not. It's not accepting reality and moving on.

I'm one to talk. It's been over five years since Sarah left, and she's as present in my thoughts as if it were yesterday. I glance back up at my mom's room. I'm not sure what to do for her.

Talking to her about seeing a therapist is like talking to a brick wall. She just shuts down. I don't want to, but I might have to move back home for a while so I can keep an eye on her.

I look up at the sound of someone knocking on my classroom door and smile when I see Christine. I set the pencil sketch I was grading down. "Hey, stranger."

It's been a week since we've had lunch together. She's been up to her eyeballs with wedding planning stuff. Brian pops his head around her, and I admit it. I'm confused. "Hey, man." They're both smiling so I think everything's okay. Christine popping by my classroom after school is not unheard of. Brian dropping by is less common. He isn't usually off of work until seven. Mr. Big, Bad Lawyer.

I look between them. "What's going on?"

They walk in holding hands, and I can tell they're up to something.

Christine glances over at Brian before starting. "We wanted to know if you'd like to have dinner with us tonight."

My eyes flick back and forth between them. "Why does this feel so formal? You could have just texted me."

Brian shrugs. "We dropped Christine's car off at the mechanic's this morning, so I left work early to pick her up. We figured we'd pop in on you since I'm here and try and get your sorry ass to have dinner with us."

It's come to this. It's a not so subtle search and rescue mission. Sure, it's been a while since I've gone out. I stop to think about it. When was the last time I went out? Six, seven months ago? I think it was sometime in the fall, and here we are, early spring.

"I need to swing past the house first. Get my mom settled."

"How about we follow you?" Brian shrugs.

He thinks he's slick. I can tell he thinks I'll bail once I get home. Truth is, I can use a night off from my mom. "Sounds good. Any place in particular you want to go?"

I flick off my desk lamp and stand while Christine and Brian bat restaurant options back and forth, finally agreeing on Indian and looking at me for my okay.

"I can go for some curry." My mom doesn't like Indian food so it'll be nice to have a change of pace.

I lock up, and the three of us walk out together. It's never stopped feeling surreal that I teach at the same place I went to middle school. These halls hold many memories, mostly good but not all. Brian's parked next to my Jetta, and true to his word, they follow me back to my mom's place. I'd finally sold my condo and moved back in with my mom.

Even though my sister, Bethany, died almost twenty years ago, her room was still exactly as it had been the day she died. It had taken my mom time, but with the exception of Bethany's room, my mom started functioning again: going to work, trying to be aware of my comings and goings. Since my dad died, we'd gone back to square one, and she doesn't seem to have any interest in functioning again. She'll shower and dress herself almost every day, but she refuses to leave the house. I know it's not healthy, and I get that I probably need to do something to push her. I'm just not sure what.

About three months ago, I brought seeing a therapist up to her. No reaction, positive or negative. Should have took it as my cue to go ahead and do it but I got caught up with work and pushed it to the back burner. A lot of good that did me, here we are three months later and I'm still dealing with it.

I hop out of my car and walk over to Brian's. He rolls down the window as I approach. "I'm just going to run in and make her a frozen dinner. Should be like five minutes. Did you two want to wait here or come inside?"

Brian glances at Christine. "We'll just hang out here."

I'm not surprised. My mom can be creepy. My house can be creepy. It feels like time has stood still in it. All through school, I wanted to be anywhere else, eventually finding a safe haven in Sarah and Brian's house. It had always been so warm and inviting over there in comparison.

I go into the kitchen, and my mom barely acknowledges my presence as I zap dinner for her. I lock up after myself and get back in my car to follow them to the restaurant. Once we're seated, Christine produces an envelope from her purse and passes it over to me.

"What's this?" I ask.

Brian slips his arm around her shoulders. "Why don't you open it and see?"

"My birthday was in December," I joke, breaking the back seal of the card.

They both watch me as I slide the card out. It doesn't take me long to figure out it's their wedding invitation. I hold it up, my inner art teacher evaluating the font and coloring. "These turned out really nice."

Our waiter stops by to take our drink orders and drops off some naan. Once he's gone, I decide to tease them, I flip the envelope over and hold it up. "What? No stamp?"

Christine shakes her head while Brian grins. "You're getting dinner, dumbass. That trumps a stupid stamp."

I shrug. "It'd be nice to get something other than bills in the mail."

"Sorry, man. You're just going to have to live with it." He laughs.

The waiter drops off our drinks and takes our orders.

Brian squeezes Christine's shoulder and rubs his jaw with his other hand. "So I have something important to ask you."

I nod.

"You and I go way back. I not only consider you a brother, but you also introduced me to the love of my life." When he says that part, Christine sighs and reaches her hand up to grasp his. They are so in love it's hard not to be happy for them. It's also hard not to find the whole thing personally depressing. Brian keeps going. "Here's the thing, man. I can't think of anyone else I'd want standing there with me. Be my best man?"

I'm stunned. I look back and forth between them as Brian and I stand to hug. "Hell, yeah, I'll be your best man."

People around us are watching and laughing, Christine included.

I feel honored, but this also means there's no way I'm getting out of going to the wedding. Not that I'd want to. It's just that part of me isn't sure what seeing Sarah will be like after all these years. Who knows? She may not even come.

9

"What time does her flight land?" I have my shoulder popped up, holding my phone to my ear as I shuffle my bags into one hand.

"Hi. Long time, man. Oh, I'm good. Thanks for asking. And Christine? She's awesome too. So cool of you to ask." There's more than a hint of sarcasm in Brian's voice.

My now free hand reaches up to grasp my phone. I clear my throat. "So when does her flight land?"

He groans. "Will, I don't know. I know she isn't flying in from Denver, and she told mom she'd just get a cab."

"A cab? Really?" I get to my gate and sit. A loud announcement blares overhead.

"Are you at the airport?" Brian asks. He must have heard the background noise.

I glance around, watching people hurry to and from the gates around me. "Yep. I'm heading to Montpelier for—"

He cuts me off. "That thing for your picture. I totally forgot that was this weekend. Christine told me you won. So what's the prize?"

"It's no big deal. Five grand. I'm donating it to the school." I scratch the back of my neck. God, I need a haircut. Got to remember to get one before the rehearsal dinner.

"What?" He grumbles. "The school? You should've put it toward another weekend in Atlantic City."

"Yeah, I'm gonna pass on that. No desire to watch you projectile vomit again," I say, shaking my head.

There's silence. "That was a great weekend."

I laugh. "What I remember of it anyway. So back to Sarah. You really don't know when she's landing?"

"Hang on a sec." I hear a muffled sound as he sets the phone down or puts his hand over it. "Sorry. Christine walked in. She says hi. Can I call you back later?"

"Sure. Tell her hi for me too," I say before hanging up.

I pull the corner of my bottom lip between my teeth and bite down as I dig through my bag of takeout. An egg sandwich and a hash brown, the breakfast of champions. I should've called Mrs. Miller. She probably would have known when Sarah is landing. I glance at my watch and decide I'll let it go. I don't like the idea of her getting a cab. Why doesn't she want someone to pick her up? She's so stubborn sometimes. God, I miss her.

HER
133

I eat my breakfast and throw the wrappers and bag away before I board. There's a guy in a suit seated next to me. I have the window. It's an early flight. As soon as we're in the air, I fall asleep. When we land, I call home to let my mom know I got here okay. I know she won't answer. She barely talks to anyone but me, and she ignores the phone when it rings. She'll listen to the answering machine, though.

"Mom, I'm in Vermont. I'll call again before I leave tomorrow." I turn off my phone and look at it in my hand for a minute. I don't know what to do about my mom. This whole situation is getting to be too much for me. Other than a weekend here and there, I can't leave her alone.

My cab ride to the hotel is short. I'm checked in to my room in no time. The ceremony is this evening, in the hotel banquet room. I flop down onto the bed. Sarah Miller is coming home. I try to think of an excuse to be at her parents' house tomorrow. I still don't know why she left. One minute, everything was fine, more than fine, perfect. Then she was gone. Over the last seven years, I've tried to move on, to find someone else. Problem is, she's it for me, and I have the next week to prove it to her.

I stand, walking over to my window. It's clear and bright out. I grab my camera from my bag and walk around taking pictures of downtown. I pop into a deli for a bite before heading back to the hotel. I packed a suit for the banquet. I shower and change before heading down. I find the organizer, and she walks me to my table.

"First time in Vermont?" she asks, smiling.

I have to think about it. I know my family vacationed in New Hampshire when I was a kid.

"I don't think so."

She gives me a long look, the kind of look with an invitation attached.

"That's a pity. Vermont can be extremely welcoming." She smiles again, putting her hand on my arm.

I nod. Not interested. I make a point to avoid her for the rest of the evening. The winning pictures are mounted and displayed around the room. There is more than one completion. My shot won the overall prize. It was a lucky shot. I keep my camera close most days. I had been leaving work and noticed a little girl had fallen off of her bike. I was walking over to help but someone beat me to it. I still had my camera bag over my shoulder, and there was something magic in the way that little boy helped her up. A glimpse at our humanity.

It was Christine who'd heard about the contest and told me to enter it. One day she'd come bursting into the teachers' lounge with a print out of the contest. She'd started as a sub for a teacher on maternity leave. She was offered the job permanently when that teacher decided not to come back after her daughter was born. We'd eat lunch together most days. She was so excited I entered. I honestly didn't think anything would come from it and was shocked when I got the letter telling me I had won. I live within my means so it wasn't like I needed the money. I teach art, and given all the budget cuts in recent years, this donation would help the kids have some newer materials and mediums to work with over the next year. There's only so far you can go with tempera paint.

It sucks that the ceremony is so close to the wedding. At least school is out. I just want more time to figure out what to say and do once Sarah is back. I only have a week to figure out what happened and what I need to do to fix it. As far as I know, she isn't dating anyone. Brian and Christine both promised she isn't bringing a plus one. My attention is pulled to the podium when my name is called. I stand, buttoning my suit jacket, and make my way up front. My speech boils down to a heartfelt thank you, and I'm presented with a fake, giant check.

On my way back to my seat, I'm stopped by the organizer. Trish, I think is her name. She gives me the actual prize check, but lets me know I can keep the giant one if I want to. The kids might get a kick out of it, but I don't want to deal with taking it on the plane. Someone else comes up to talk to me or her. It's hard to tell, and I make my escape.

I head back to my room. My flight leaves early tomorrow. I don't have a direct flight like I did today. I have to change planes in Newark. A perfect symphony of shit the next morning almost makes me miss my connection. I'm one of the last people to board in Newark. After the attendant finishes up her flight speech, I pull out a book. The turn off electronics light comes on, and I watch the people with tablets and ereaders groan as they turn them off around me. Score one for old school, I think to myself, turning a page. I'm a couple of pages in when I get the feeling someone is watching me. I glance back out of curiosity, and for a moment, I wonder if I'm imagining things.

Is it really her?

I'm not sure if I trust my voice. Just be cool, man. "No way. Sarah. Sarah Miller?"

She nods. She's smiling at me. I'm unbuckling my belt and asking to trade seats with the woman across the aisle from her before I know what I'm doing. The guy on the other side of her offers to get up as well so we can sit right next to each other. After I sit, she leans towards me to put her purse under the seat in front of her. My teeth clamp down on the corner of my lip. A lock of her hair falls forward. Her hand moves to tuck it behind her ear, but I beat her. I swear her eyes dilate when my fingertip grazes her earlobe.

She looks amazing. She's morphed into my grown up fantasy. Part of me wants to pull her into my lap and kiss every inch of her, but I'm pretty sure that might get me kicked off the plane. I'm not sure what to say to her. I'm not sure if I even believe she's here, on my plane. Stick to neutral stuff, I think before asking her how she's been.

Her voice takes me back in time. I'm not sure what I'm going to have to do, but I will do whatever it takes to win her back. I try not to lose myself in her chocolate eyes. For someone who had such power over me, she never seemed like she knew it. We're talking about work when she laughs. I love that sound. I used to pin her down and tickle her. Sure it was an excuse to touch her, but I loved the way she laughed. She could never hold back and giggle. She was always full powered.

I make the mistake of telling her, and she argues, bringing up the time she snorted root beer out of her nose. I can't believe I'd forgotten about that. Her eyes widen as I laugh. That's another thing I can't remember: the last time I was as happy as I am now with her.

I ask her about her job, even though I already know. I've been pumping Brian for information for years. I don't want to sound like some crazy stalker so I act like I don't know. I just want her to keep talking. If she does, maybe she'll remember how we were.

I'm going to hell for lying. "So what brings you out this way? Work?"

"Nope. Brian's getting married."

I act like I don't know. When she jokes about moms going crazy over losing their baby boys, I know she means my mom. I do, but I don't want to tell her about my dad. I worry the side of my lip between my teeth. It's an old habit I barely notice I do anymore. I only notice this time because I watch her eyes drop to my mouth. Here goes.

"My dad passed a couple years ago."

Her eyes soften, and she puts her hand on my arm. I look down at it. She doesn't even know she still owns me. She asks about my mom, and finally, after she tells me I'm a good son, she moves her hand. The attendant comes by to pass out drinks. I question her drink choice before I bring up the day she left.

"It was just like one minute you were there and then…" I shrug. What I don't say is, why did you leave me?

She looks down and spins a ring on her thumb. It takes me less than a second to recognize that ring. I grab her hand and pull it up before looking at her.

"I can't believe you still have this ring." Thinking that has to mean something.

She tugs her hand from mine and covers it with her other hand, but I don't even care. She is still wearing the ring I gave her over a decade ago. That has to mean something. It means, whether she knows it or not, that she is still mine.

10

She agrees to let me drive her home. She may kill me when we get to her house, but I'm still taking it as a good sign. I send a text to Brian to give him a heads up. I also tell him I didn't tell her I know about the wedding. He sends back a picture off the internet of a donkey laughing. Dork. I think what he's trying to tell me is he is going to laugh his ass off when Sarah finds out I know about the wedding.

I look at her, and she looks uncomfortable. I glance at my watch out of habit. A rush of words come out of her mouth. She feels bad for keeping me. She can just take Marta or a cab.

"Sarah, don't be silly. I'm not letting you get a cab."

Her mouth quirks up at one corner. "You're not letting me?"

I smirk at her.

She rolls her eyes. "Fine. Wait. Just don't be so bossy."

I can't help myself. I pull her into my arms. I tell her how much I've missed her while I breathe her in. She smells like pears. I've never craved one so bad in my life. As we wait for her bags, I catch her looking at me a couple times. That has to be a good thing. When I see her reach for a red bag, I grab it for her. Once she has both her bags, she follows me out to the parking lot. I'm popping open the trunk when I hear her laugh behind me.

"Another freaking Jetta?"

I look back at her. "They're good cars."

I have to hold back a laugh when she asks if she can press the button.

I lean towards her. "Anytime, Miller Lite."

As we drive to her house, I point out all the things that changed. I want her to see that, even after all of this time and even though things changed, they can still feel the same between us. I still need to find out why she left in the first place. I know no matter what it is we can get past it. When we get to her house, she asks me what I'm doing to fix the parts of me that make unhappy. I tell her the truth.

"I'm working on it. I got you in my car again."

Oh shit. Why did I just say that? She looks like she's about to hyperventilate and not in a good way. I back peddle like a bitch.

"I just mean that I've missed you in my life."

That doesn't help. She gets out and walks around back to the trunk. I smack my head on the steering wheel before going back to get her bags out. She tries to ask me if I should be heading home. Her mouth drops when I walk right into her house. She stumbles after me. I leave her bags in the living room. I can hear people in the kitchen so I head that way.

"She's going to kill you," Brian says in my ear as he pats me on the back.

I lean in to kiss her mom on the cheek and catch her eye. Sarah doesn't look pissed, just confused. I walk around the table and grab an apple. Her mouth drops.

She points at me. "He's eating an apple."

Her mom looks at her. "So?"

I might as well fess up. I brush past her to toss the apple core in the trash. "Just because you left doesn't mean I did."

"I didn't know." Her voice is so small I want to just pull her into my arms.

When Brian tells her I introduced him to Christine and I'm the best man in the wedding, she turns on her heel and races out of the room. I chase her up to her room. She asks how I know Christine. She's pissed but starts laughing when I tell her Christine teaches math at Renfroe. Only Sarah can go from one extreme to another like that, and I love it. She flops onto her bed, giving me an excuse to come over and sit next to her. First day back, and I'm already sitting on her bed with her. I must be doing something right. Until she kicks me out.

I head back downstairs and talk to Brian for a while before heading home. I'll be back in a few hours for dinner. I check on my mom first. It's good to see she's gotten dressed. The last time I went out of town overnight, she was still in her nightgown when I got home. I remember things being bad like this right after my sister died. I just don't think it took her this long to move past it, not that she'll ever fully move past it. It's just that she was able to go back to work after a few months. Our house never felt like it did before Bethany died. Her room still creeps me out. Not one thing has moved since that day.

My mom is the only one who ever went in there after, to vacuum and dust. It feels like a tomb. The first time I ever went to Sarah's house, I felt like I could finally relax. Her family just folded me into them. It never felt like I was a guest.

My mom is in the living room looking at old photo albums. I leave her. There's no point telling her to stop, even though they upset her. All she'll do is make me sit with her and look at them as well. I loved my dad. We weren't as close as Brian or even I am with his dad. He seemed lost after my sister died and didn't know what to do for my mom. I think he used work as an escape from this house. I barely saw him outside of family vacations and even then he'd find a way to disappear.

I unpack before jumping into the shower. I can't stop thinking about Sarah. Up until now, it had just been this idea that she would be home for the wedding. This anticipation that I knew I would see her again. That moment at the airport, when I held her in my arms again, I just can't wait to do it again. I take my time shaving and feel like a girl when I mess with my hair. God, why am I nervous? Once I'm dressed, I pace around my room. I'm not supposed to be there for another hour. I go down to check on my mom again.

She looks at my clothes. "You aren't staying for dinner?"

I shake my head. "No, mom. Remember it's Brian's wedding this week. There's a bridal party dinner tonight."

Her face falls. "But you weren't home for dinner last night either."

I hate it when she tries to guilt trip me. "I can make you something before I go and hang out with you while you eat."

She closes her eyes and nods like that's the least I could do. She follows me into the kitchen. I boil some pasta and sauté a chicken breast in another pan. My grandmother would probably turn over in her grave, but I top it off with some spaghetti sauce from a jar. My mom eats sitting on a stool at the island while I clean up the mess I've made. We don't talk. I'm not even sure why she wants me around. Either way, it's a welcome distraction to kill time. I kiss her on the cheek when I hear Brian honk from the driveway.

"Where's Christine?" I ask, hopping in.

He lifts his brows. "The girls are getting ready together at my folks' place."

Christine has been known to take her time when it comes to getting ready. It makes me wonder about Sarah. She never seemed to care about all of that. "Wanna make a bet on if they're ready or not when we get there?"

He shakes his head. "Nope. That'd be a stupid bet."

We're halfway to his house before he asks me about Sarah.

"What do you want to know?"

He taps on the steering wheel while we wait at a traffic signal. "I know you're still interested in her. All I ask is that you not piss her off before my wedding."

"Hey—"

He cuts me off. "Look, I don't need to know exactly what went down between you two. You're both grownups. That's all I'm going to say on it."

I nod as we pull into his old neighborhood. Neither of us are shocked to find out the girls aren't ready. It's cool, though, because we only have to wait like five minutes before they come down. We stand when they walk into the room. Christine is two steps ahead of Sarah and blocks my view for a moment. When she moves over to say something to Brian, I gulp. I'm not even sure how to deal with how fucking hot she looks right now. I'm slightly embarrassed by the thoughts of what I would do to her that are flashing across my mind right now.

I'm not sure where to look. Her legs looks like my favorite wet dream but her face. God, she's beautiful. She knows I'm watching her. Shit, I can't take my eyes off her.

I try to make a joke. "Got everything you need?" And I'll be damned if she didn't forget her ID. I try to discretely watch her ass as she hauls it up the stairs to get her ID from another bag. When she comes back down, Brian offers Christine his arm to walk her out to his car. I do the same and can't help but feel put out when Sarah shakes her head and walks past me. What the hell? She can't hold my arm? Did I piss her off again?

Christine sits upfront so Sarah and I are in the back. I try to catch her eye more than once. She has to be ignoring me. I had a picture of how tonight was going to go in my head, and this is not it. When we get to the restaurant, she's seated next to Brian and across from me. We order a bunch of food to eat family style. While we wait for the food, I help myself to the bread and dip on our table. A waiter comes up to see if anyone wants to try the sangria. I'm more of a beer guy so I don't try any. I'm fucking hypnotized when Sarah does. Our eyes lock as she parts her lips. The sangria is in a leather pouch that the waiter squeezes, shooting a stream of wine into her mouth.

It's fucking erotic to watch. I drop my napkin in my lap and have to adjust myself before anyone notices I'm sporting a semi. God, what I want to do to her mouth. When she looks away, I brush my calf against her leg. Her eyes flick back to mine. I hold them as I pop a piece of bread in my mouth, hoping she can tell what I want to do to her. When I lick some oil off my finger, she jumps up, excusing herself to go to the bathroom. Brian gives me a look as I follow her. I wait for her, just outside the door.

She's surprised to see me when she comes out but plays it off. "Long line for the men's room?" She tries to move past me.

Not so fast, I think grabbing her wrist. Her back is to me. Why doesn't she turn around?

"Sarah," I plead.

The anger in her voice surprises me when she snaps. "What are you playing at, Will?"

"Playing?" Now I'm pissed. I give her arm a tug, and she turns to face me. "I promise you this is no game."

"Alright." Her voice is cold. "What do you want from me?"

This is it, my shot. "Everything." I slide my hands up her arms and hold them right below her shoulders. "I want everything from you."

Her eyes look wet, but it's hard to tell. "I gave you everything once. Now I have nothing else for you."

She pulls away with little effort. I'm too stunned by what she's said to hold on. I've let her get away again. She sits back down and looks up at me. I haven't moved. I'm still trying to figure out what the fuck just happened. I just made it clear I still want her, but she made it seem like she was the injured party. What the hell? She left me. I still don't have a fucking clue why, but I still want her no matter what. I walk back to the table. I need to figure out a way to get her to talk to me. I'm obviously missing something.

She avoids my eyes at dinner. Afterward, we all head to a local dance club. I know any chance to get her to talk to me tonight has probably passed. Part of me feels like if I can get her to relax, maybe dance with me, she'll figure out I'm serious. Christine pulls her and the other girls out onto the dance floor. I can't take my eyes off of her. When we were dating, we were both so young. It's cool to see how she's matured. How confident she looks in her skin. I gnaw on the inside of my lip when I see other guys watching her too. It's stupid to be jealous, but part of me wants to deck any other guy looking at her.

One guy in particular is really starting to piss me off. I stiffen as I watch him approach her and try to dance with her. His hands go for her hips, and I can't stop myself. I'm at her side, taking her hand, letting him know she's with me. She doesn't fight me as I lead her to another part of the dance floor.

"I was taking care of it," she says, pulling her hand from mine.

"I know," I shrug, "I was just looking for an excuse to dance with you."

She tells me she won't dance with me then leaves me in the middle of the dance floor. Like a dumbass, I follow her. She's using Brian as a shield so I give her space. Partly for her but mainly for the tap dance she's doing on my ego. I avoid her the rest of the night, curious if she'll make any attempt to talk to me. It sucks that she doesn't. Brian and Christine drop her off first. Once she's out of the car, Christine turns back to look at me.

"You two used to date, right?"

I nod.

"There was so much sexual tension coming off the both of you; I felt dirty for watching."

"Chris, really?" Brian looks ill. "That's my kid sister."

She waves him off and looks back at me. "So? What's the deal?"

Brian's eyes flick to mine through the rearview mirror. When I shrug, he looks back at the road.

"Honestly, I don't know. I wanted a chance to talk to her, but she seems pissed at me for something. Problem is, I have no fucking clue what it is."

"You want her, though, don't you?" She's gripping the arm rest as she looks back at me.

I exhale. "Only for the last seven years."

Her eyes light up.

I point at her. "Promise me you won't say a word."

She bobs her head up and down, grinning while Brian shakes his. She sees him out of the corner of her eye and smacks his arm. He was right to shake his head. I don't know what possessed me to tell her. She can't keep a secret.

The lights are out when we pull up to my house. Brian stays in the driveway with his lights on long enough for me to get into the house. I glance down at my watch. We were out later than I thought. I lock up and head straight to bed. I have to be back at the Millers' tomorrow to help make a slide show for the rehearsal dinner.

It takes me a while to fall asleep. I can't get the look Sarah gave me before she walked away from me at the restaurant out of my head. What happened? She seemed cool on the plane. Was she really this upset that I didn't tell her I knew about the wedding? That doesn't seem like a big enough deal. There has to be something else; I just have to figure out what it is.

11

Brian asks me to stop by and help them pick out pictures for a slideshow to play at the rehearsal dinner. He calls me before I leave to see what kind of sub I want. I pull up right as they're walking in the house. I'm maybe five steps behind them. I let myself in and head to the kitchen. Sarah is trying to deep throat her sub. Only girl I ever knew who could look hot stuffing her face. Her brown hair is in a messy bun on the top of her head, and she's bumming it in a pair of yoga pants and a tank top. I'll never get over how beautiful she is. When she sees me, she blushes and covers her mouth.

I look away so she can chew without me watching her. Her Uncle Chip is there, and I lean in to give him and hug. He was always cool to me.

"You didn't wait for me?" I ask, sitting next to her. I know I'm being a punk, but I can't help it around her.

"Only Sarah couldn't wait," her mom replies.

"My mother only mentioned Brian and Christine were coming." She looks at her mom. "Thanks, mom. Really, thank you."

Shit, she didn't know I was coming. "It's cool. Brian thought you might need my help with the slideshow."

She glares at Brian. "What? Why would you think that? I can handle making a slideshow."

Great. "I can go." I start to stand up.

Her hand wraps around my arm as she tugs me down. I allow her to pull me even if she won't look at me. Sarah always was stubborn. This is as close as I'll get to an invitation, and I'll take it. She's quiet during lunch. I wonder what she's thinking, if she can tell how much she still affects me. How I have to make myself look away from her.

After lunch, Brian, Christine, Sarah, and I set up in the living room. I can't keep my eyes off her ass in those pants. I distractedly follow her before I remember I need my computer. I grab my laptop bag from the foyer. I brought my computer and my scanner. Christine brought pictures of herself from when she was a baby until before she met Brian. I guess she wants similar pictures of Brian to go with them. They start flipping through photo albums while I start scanning the pictures she brought. They're all pointing out pictures here and there, the really good ones they take out and give to me. I have a stack of like twenty to scan when it gets really quiet.

I look up and see Brian and Christine looking at Sarah. She's holding this faded brown leather album. The kind that has the paper that is sticky and there is a clear sheet of plastic you can pull back to move the pictures around. Silent tears are streaming down her cheeks. Awareness hits her, and she sets the album on the coffee table before hurrying out of the room. Brian starts to get up, but I stop him. Setting my laptop on a side table I follow her, pausing only to look at the page that upset her so much.

It's a picture of the three of us playing Uno, must have been freshman year. She's looking at me with a dreamy, far away expression. I want to shake my former self for not figuring it out sooner. I follow her to the kitchen. Her back is to me, and she has a glass of water in her hand.

"Sarah."

"Please," she says quietly, her voice breaking.

I know she wants to be alone, but I just can't leave her like this. "Can we talk?"

The slight tremor to her shoulders is the only sign that she's still crying. I want to wrap my arms around her and make whatever is hurting her go away. I might never know what made her leave, but none of that will even matter if I can just get her to talk to me. A hand settles on my shoulder, and I almost jump out of my skin. I turn, my eyes connecting with Chip's. He looks at Sarah then back at me before motioning for me to go. I gulp. She needs someone right now, and I want to be that person for her. I hesitate, looking at her again.

He cocks his head at me in a silent dare. I guess today is just not the day.

I slowly walk back into the living room. Brian and Christine ask about her, and I let them know Chip is with her. Brian had gathered a healthy pile of pictures to go along with Christine's. Rather than stay and scan them there, I take them with me. I need to get out of this house. This may be the first time I've ever felt like that.

The Millers' house has always felt like a sanctuary for me. I don't want to be at my house either. Right now, I miss my condo. I drive around and try to clear my head. It isn't working. This town is a topographical memory lane. Some days, like today, it's harder to see certain places and not be blindsided by memories. I give up and drive home. Luckily, my mom isn't in the living room when I walk past. I get to my room and lock the door before I feel some of the tension roll off of me. This week isn't going how I pictured it would. Somehow, it's going in the opposite direction I wanted it to. Sarah talked to me more the first day I saw her. I just can't figure out why she's upset with me.

After dinner, I meet Brian for a drink. Christine is stressing over last minute details and tells him to get out of her hair. I envy the fact that they have no problem talking to each other. I miss what Sarah and I once had. It might be crazy to still be hung up on the girl I dated my senior year of high school, but she was so much more than that. She was my best friend. Brian is no help when I ask about her.

He shakes his glass before taking a long swallow. "She didn't come out of her room. Uncle Chip talked to her and said to leave her alone."

"Were you going to talk to her?" I wipe the condensation off my drink with a bar napkin.

"I was," he starts. "She's my sister. I want to know what's bugging her." He looks at me. "Do you still?"

I nod. I know what he's asking. Do I still love his baby sister? I've never loved anyone else.

"You two just need to talk."

I blink at him. "I'm not fucking stupid. I've been trying to talk to her since she got back."

He has the decency to look sorry. "She can be stubborn." He laughs. "When we were little I used to sit on her until she would listen."

"I don't see that working this time." I wipe the condensation off my glass with my thumb.

He leans his elbows on the bar and nods. "It'd be funny but..." He just shakes his head.

I take another drink. "So two days, man. How's Christine holding up?"

He looks up at the ceiling. "She's no—what's that show? Bridezilla? But she is stressed. I can't wait until it's just the two of us."

"Why's she stressing?"

He just shakes his head. "She wanted this one caterer, which, whatever. It's cool, right? Only we could have just had the country club cater it but didn't because she wanted this other place." He pauses. "I'm not saying I wanted them to cater it. I just think it would have been one less thing to worry about if they did and now the caterer we got is saying there are issues with the space."

I nod but only because I have zero opinion about anything he just said.

He sees it as permission to keep going. "She's been on the phone with the caterer, on the phone with the club, on the phone with the caterer and the club. Each call, she just gets more stressed and—" He takes another drink. "God love her if I try and help and whatever I do is wrong."

I lift my glass and say the only thing that seems fitting at the moment. "Women."

Brian chuckles as he bumps my glass with his. "Women."

"Well, let her know I got all the pictures scanned and set the background song she wanted to loop. I loaded it on to a flash drive. She said the restaurant runs them off a mini laptop."

He pulls out his cell phone and starts sending a text. He looks over at me and shrugs. "Knowing there's one less thing to worry about will cheer her up."

"And you had to tell her right this second?" I ask, gesturing to his phone.

He hits the send button and grins. "Why make her wait when I know I can make her happy right now."

It's not a question. It's a statement. Brian and Christine aren't perfect, but they have it figured out. Whatever they do, they still think about how it will affect each other first. Other than my parents, the only person I have ever done that for is Sarah. I would do anything to make her smile. She was the same way. We had this balance of putting each other first. I'll never forget how I felt when it all went away.

12

When she walks in the room, it's like someone somewhere pressed a giant mute button. I can't take my eyes off of her. She's wearing this clingy, dark grey dress. Her hair is curled, the top part pulled back, and her legs…I could stare at those all night. It's been years, but I will never be able to deny my attraction to her. Her Uncle Chip walks her over to our table. I see her blush, knowing I'm watching her.

Brian told me earlier she had a migraine yesterday. "How are you feeling?"

"Um, better. Thank you." She won't look me in the eyes.

"I just—"

She gives her head a little shake. "Don't."

I can't. "Wanted to tell you how beautiful I think you look tonight."

She looks down at her hands and spins her ring. It has to mean something that she's still wearing it, especially here. "Thank you."

I wish she would look at me. I ask her what happened the other day. She hesitates and tries to say it was nothing, but we both know that's bullshit.

"Sarah—"

Her eyes move to something or someone behind me. She stands, starts to move past me. "Excuse me."

I don't want to let her escape. I grab her wrist, stopping her. She stares at my hand. I can just barely feel her pulse racing. When neither of us says anything, she finally looks at me. I can't find the words to fix whatever happened. Her eyes are wide. She has to know how I feel. Why does she seem so scared? When she shakes her head, I drop my hand.

I'm losing my mind; we're at the rehearsal dinner. Christine would kick my ass if I made some scene. That doesn't mean I I'm not going to try and get her to talk to me. I'm just going to try and be a bit more discreet about it. I'm curious why she's getting up. I turn my head and see she's heading towards Brian and Christine.

I grin and stand, catching up to her quickly. Just before she reaches them, I've caught her and stand next to her, resting my hand on the small of her back. I hear her let out a small gasp. That's right. We both know I still affect her. I keep my face neutral.

I don't want to piss her off. Sarah talks to Christine while Brian gives me a 'what the hell' look. I shrug. I watch powerless as Christine grabs her hand and leads her away to introduce her to people. My hand hesitates midair, pining over the loss of her warmth before I let it fall to my side.

Brian stands next to me, and we watch them make their way around the room. "Sarah looked uncomfortable. Don't be pissing off my baby sister right before my wedding."

I look at him. "I'm not trying to piss her off, but at some point, she's going to tell me why she left." I pause and look up at the ceiling. "Whether it pisses her off or not."

He gives me a warning look. "Don't make me regret I invited you."

I grin. "Hey, don't forget who introduced you."

He smirks, and we walk back to the table.

I have every intention of leaving her alone. I do. It's just that she's sitting right next to me. I don't know how to not touch her. I shift in my seat and touch her leg with mine. I must have caught her off guard because she flinches and drops her fork. It clangs loudly against her plate, and everyone at the table looks at her. I unsuccessfully try not to laugh. When she elbows me, it feels like old times.

I lean towards her, my lips a breath away from my ear. "I knew you would touch me at some point," I tease.

When I lean back in my chair, she looks at me. "It was my elbow," she argues.

I shrug. I'll take what I can get. "Still counts."

She narrows her eyes. "That does not count."

I wet my lips. "It does, and now you're talking to me too."

I'm not trying to make her angry. I'm just trying to get past whatever bullshit she's putting between us.

She takes a deep breath. "I don't understand why you're doing this."

I'm confused. "Doing what?"

"This." She practically growls, waving her hand between us.

I still love her, but man, I may never understand what goes on in her head. "What? Talking to you?"

She groans, then notices Brian watching us and lowers her voice. "Acting like nothing happened."

"I'm not acting like nothing happened." She's the one trying to act like we have no history.

"Then what are you doing?" she snaps.

I have to lean back while my dinner plate is taken away. "I just want you to talk to me."

When she rolls her eyes and tells me she's talking to me right now, I restrain the urge to put her over my knee. I roll my shoulders before I look into those fiery eyes of hers. "No, you're not. Sitting there, rolling your eyes. You might be hearing the words I'm saying, but we are not talking."

She closes her eyes. "I seriously don't understand what you're trying to say."

I start to say something but stop when the slideshow starts. I've already seen it so I watch her and then Brian and Christine watching it. The love in their eyes, what they have. Can't she see that should be us? I lean forward to say something but pull back when the server starts setting the dessert plates in front of us.

I'm not hungry, I watch her eat instead. I wonder if she's picturing my heart the way she stabs at her cheesecake. I push my plate away. I've decided I'm dropping everything for the rest of the night. Then she makes a little moan sound as she eats.

Fuck this. I lean into her, making her jump. "Sarah, can we talk outside?"

I don't know why she agrees, but I start to relax. Finally, I can figure out what the hell made her leave. I stand and watch as she takes a drink of her water before offering her my hand. She refuses it so I motion for her to go first. I put my hand on the small of her back, cursing the material keeping me away from her skin. I direct her to a back door. I've been here before. There's a deck with a path leading off of it closer to the lake. I know there's a bench down there where we can talk in peace.

She sits first, and I sit right next to her only for her to move away. I look down at the space between us, trying to figure out why she's acting like this before looking out over the dark water. I can feel her eyes on me. I'm the one who asked her down here to talk, and now I can't think of anything to say.

She breaks the silence for me. "The slideshow was beautiful, Will."

My head is telling me to thank her, to kiss her, to do anything but say what I'm about to. "Sarah, why did you leave?"

She closes her eyes and shakes her head. I turn and cup her cheek with my hand. For the briefest moment, she starts to lean into my hand, and I feel this sense of hope. It's gone less than a second later when she jerks away from my touch. It happens so fast I blink at my hand before I lower it. It's warm out, but she shivers and rubs her hands up and down her upper arms. I shrug off my jacket and feel that hope again when she leans forward so I can drape it over her shoulders.

I open my mouth to ask her again when she stands, walking a few steps closer to the lake. I follow her. I'm about to put my arms around her when she turns to look at me. I don't know why, but she pulls my jacket off and thrusts it to me with one word on her lips. "Jessica."

I'm too floored by what she said to go after her. I stand there, stunned as I watch her go back into the restaurant. What the hell did Jessica have to do with Sarah leaving? It just doesn't make any sense to me. I walk back to the bench and sit, my jacket now lying across my lap. I can hear muffled sounds of conversation coming from inside, but the beat of the water lapping the posts of the dock down the way are louder.

The buzz and chirps of nighttime insects are louder than even the water. I'm dazed. That was the last thing I ever expected to come out of her mouth. I glance back towards the party. I just don't feel up to talking to anyone or acting like I'm fine. I'm not fine.

I feel like I'm trying to figure out a puzzle that has no solution. I stand, skipping the back door and heading to the side of the building. I run into Chip sneaking a smoke with one of the waitresses. He tries to hold it behind his back so I don't see. I could care less right now. I try to just nod and make my way past him, but he stops me, cocking his head towards the building so the waitress will get the hint and leave. After she does, he drops his smoke, stepping on it to put it out.

He points to the butt. "That's between me and you."

I nod, hoping that's all he wants from me.

It isn't. "Where are you off to in such a hurry?"

I jam my hands in my pockets and focus on a brick on the wall behind him. "Just need to take off. Can you tell—" I hesitate. Who do I want him to tell? "Brian that I'm not feeling great so that's why I'm leaving?" It's the truth. I feel like shit.

He nods. "Is that really why you're leaving? Or does it have something to do with Sarah?"

I shrug. He can read whatever he wants to into that. I've got too much shit running through my head to care right now. He nods again and doesn't say anything when I leave this time. I sit in my car for a couple minutes before I turn it on and leave.

If I knew how to get a hold of Jessica, I'd probably be interrogating her right now. Last I heard, she was working at Crate and Barrel. What just happened is like a loop in my head, Sarah's face, her expression as she said it. Something happened. I just don't know what.

The house is dark when I get home. I'm relieved. I just don't think I can handle anything else tonight. I even swipe one of my mom's sleeping pills. Otherwise, I'll be up all night, and I'm supposed to help Brian over at the church in the morning. It kills me, but the last thing I picture before I pass out is the look in her eyes.

The next morning, I have breakfast with my mom, reminding her that today's the wedding so I might just crash at the hotel if it goes late. It's like talking to a wall. No nod, no grunt. I'm not even sure if she knows I'm here half of the time. I shake it off, but I know she's getting worse, and by doing nothing, I'm enabling her. I just don't know what to do. I pity her, and I know pushing her in any direction will be painful for her. She hasn't been the best mom over the years, but she's had to deal with more than most.

As I walk past her, I place my hand over hers and give it a squeeze. I shower and throw on an old t-shirt and some soccer shorts. I have my tux in the car. Brian is waiting for me when I pull up.

"Feeling better?"

I nod; I still don't want to get into it.

Brian has other plans. He stops me as I go to move past him. "Sarah said something kinda cryptic last night. I just need to know if you ever did anything to hurt her."

My mouth drops. "What did she say?"

He starts pacing in front of me. "She came by the condo to see it last night, and when I'm driving her home, I bring you up and I think I said that this whole thing was hurting you or something like that." Then he stops to look at me. "So she replies you don't get to hurt. That sounds like some serious shit to me. What the hell happened between you two?"

I need to sit down. I lower myself to the stairs, shaking my head. "I have no fucking clue. That's the whole thing, Brian. She took off without a word, and I still have no fucking clue what happened. I asked her last night and all she would say was Jessica, but I don't know what that means. Did Jessica do something that Sarah is blaming me for? I don't get to hurt? Why does she get to decide that? I've been hurting for the last seven years.

She's the one that took off, not me." I get up and start to walk back to my car.

Brian runs after me. "Come on, man. Don't go."

I turn and face him. I'm pissed. He can tell.

"Look, man. I believe you. I don't know what Sarah thinks happened, but I need you standing next to me today. So what do you need? Want a shot? Need a cigarette? What?"

I rub my hand across my face. "I have no fucking clue."

He grins, trying to hold back a laugh. "I've heard flower arranging can be calming."

I didn't. "Did you so say flower arranging?"

He snorts, and damn it, I smile.

He puts his arms around my shoulder and turns us both to face the church. "I've got a shitload of floral sprays in the trunk of my car that somehow need to make it into the ring at the end of every pew. I sure as shit am not doing them all by myself."

I bite down on the side of my mouth while I think it over, absentmindedly rubbing my tongue across it and the back of my teeth before I answer him. "Wanna race?"

He flexes. "That's my best man."

I shake my head and laugh. Almost any pain in the ass chore is more fun if you turn it into a competition. We cart in all the boxes of flowers and divide them equally. We both start at the front of the church. We didn't count the flower things but there doesn't look like there are enough to do both sides of every pew in the church.

By starting at the main aisle, we'll hit the most important sides and then start over at the front of the church on the other side if there are any left. Brian does the countdown and then we're off. He trips and falls halfway, and it takes me a minute to stop laughing at him and make him promise not to break anything before the wedding. Because of his quick recovery, he wins. We manage to do the main aisle and half of the other sides.

"Man I need another shower," I say, trying to get some air to flow under my shirt.

"You can hop in the shower at the house."

I hesitate." Will Sarah be there?"

He shakes his head. "They went up early to have their hair and makeup done at a salon. Then they're getting dressed at Christine's mom's place."

I follow him back to the house. Chip and Mr. Miller are drinking coffee in the kitchen. Brian stops me from taking a shower after his dad tells him Sarah's wedding present is in the back of his car. I end up riding with Brian back to his place to help him carry it up. When we get there and open the back, I laugh. Brian looks at me like I've lost my mind.

I shake my head. "We got you the same tables, bud. Your sister and I each bought one piece to a matched set."

We have to rush to get back and showered, so we don't talk much. Once we're back at his folk's house, I wave at Chip and Mr. M before heading upstairs to shower. I see Sarah's stuff all over the place. She was never very organized. In the shower, I'm like an addict looking for a hit. I open her bottle of conditioner and inhale pears. God, that smells good. I always liked the fruity smells more than the flowery stuff girls sometimes wear. I take a fast shower. Brian wants the shower so I get dressed in Sarah's room.

After my conversation with Brian this morning, I'm not going to let her run off again like she did. As soon as the wedding is over, she's telling me what happened. What did Jessica have to do with her leaving?

13

I follow Mr. M in my car as we drive back to the church. They didn't choose separate ushers so the other groomsmen and I seat people as they show up. Brian is at the front of the church going over some last minute stuff with the pastor. We get the heads up from Mrs. M that the limo dropped the girls off at the side entrance and they'll wait for Christine's dad to collect them to start the procession. Brian walks over to us, catching the tail end of the conversation and rushes off with his mom hot on his heels. I'd follow him, but I just got tapped to escort Christine's grandmother down the aisle.

When Brian gets back, he walks Christine's mom to her seat while Mr. and Mrs. M walk behind them to their seats. After that, we all line up at the front and wait for the music to start.

"Where'd you go?" I ask out the side of my mouth.

"I went and talked to Chris." He grins.

The ring bearer and flower girl are the kids of the maid of honor and one of the groomsmen and come out first. The guests all ohh and ahh over how cute they are. Yes, they're cute, but I'm only interested in seeing Sarah. Time slows when she steps out. I don't think I'll ever get used to how beautiful she is. Her bridesmaid dress is pale blue, the same shade as the flower on my lapel.

Instead of falling past her shoulders, her brown hair is up; jeweled pins catch the light from overhead as she makes her way down the aisle. Our eyes lock, and all I can think is one day I hope our eyes lock as she walks down the aisle when she's the bride becoming my wife.

I watch the ceremony feeling detached. It should be us up there. When it's over, Justine, Christine's best friend and maid of honor, and I follow Brian and Christine out of the church, and the photographer tells us to wait there for pictures. I wait for Sarah to come out and can't stop myself from going to her. I hold out my hand to her and relax when she takes it.

My fingers brush back and forth across her skin. "You look beautiful, Sarah."

"Thank you. You look," she gulps, "nice too."

As though she finally realizes she's in my grasp, she starts to pull away. I look down at her and shake my head. I don't want to let her go. When one of the bridesmaids comes to collect her to go back inside for some pictures, I pause before I can do it. I watch while their pictures are taken, and then there are some pictures of just the groomsmen. When they do group shots, I relax when she's back in my arms. I don't let go of her this time.

We're on the church steps, and I notice her looking around. After a moment, she looks up at me. "I'm supposed to ride with my parents."

I chew on the inside of my lip. This is probably going to piss her off. "I already talked to them. You're riding with me."

"What?"

She heard me. I shrug. "I need to talk, and you need to listen. Pretty sure you won't jump out of a moving car."

She rolls her eyes. "My clutch?"

I keep her arm in mine and walk her back to the room where the girls left their stuff before the ceremony. Once she has it, we walk back out to my car. I open her door for her and close it once she's in. I slowly walk around to my side, and part of me wonders if I'm ready for whatever she's about to tell me.

I don't say anything until I'm on the road. "Sarah, what did Jessica have to do with you leaving?"

Her arms are folded across her chest. "I thought you were going to talk and I was supposed to listen."

I'm sick of her fighting this. "Please answer me."

"What? You're so surprised I found out?"

I look at her, pissed. "Alright, let me just say this one time. I have no idea what you are talking about."

She starts spinning her ring. "So are you trying to say Jessica didn't go with you to Italy?"

I turn into the parking lot of the country club where the reception is being held. Shit. Wasn't expecting that. "She did, but—"

She cuts me off as I park. "Don't, just don't."

I watch in a daze, and she opens the door and books it across the parking lot. I shake my head before I go after her and watch as she dashes into the ladies' room. I would have followed her if our old principal wasn't standing in the lobby giving me a weird look. This has to be a new low. Sarah is hiding from me in a bathroom. I need a drink. I look at the door one last time before I head inside the ballroom. Maybe fifteen minutes later, I don't see her, but I know she's there. I have my arm slung across the back of her chair.

"Fall in?" She doesn't answer so I keep going. "So I went over with Brian this morning to help pick your wedding gift. Pretty big coincidence out of everything they registered for, we picked the same thing."

I tilt my head back and look up at her before pulling her chair out for her to sit. She flags down a server and orders a drink. She's shutting me out, and I'm starting to wonder if it's even worth it to try and figure out what's going on in that head of hers. The DJ announces the arrival of the new Mr. and Mrs. Miller. We all stand and applaud, and we all sit when Justine goes to give her toast. Shit. Best Man. I need to make a toast. I stand when it's my turn and stay where I am.

I look down at Sarah and take a deep breath before I start. "I work with Christine and have known Brian forever. He saw me having lunch with Christine one day and had to meet her. In our infinite wisdom, we came up with a plan to get them together. It was clear there was something there when Brian called me after their first date and could not stop talking about her. He told me he thought she was the one.

I remember telling him to tell her that, to make sure she knew everyday just how much he loved her and how she was the only one for him. Don't make the mistake I did and let the one get away. He took my advice and almost scared her away by coming on too strong. Moral of the story, given my romantic history, is they are clearly meant for each other, considering I got involved and they're still together."

I sit back down and know, no matter what, I have to do everything in my power to get Sarah back. She's stubborn and a giant pain in the ass sometimes, but she's the only girl I've ever loved and I'd be a dumbass if I stop trying. After the first few dances, Brian walks over and asks her to dance.

I give them a couple of minutes before I decide to cut in. I see her shake her head. but I think Brian's on my side and has already put her hands in mine. This time, she doesn't run away. I slide my hand around her waist and pull her to my chest. I love how she feels in my arms and pull her even tighter when she rests her head on my shoulder.

I don't want to chase her anymore. Can't she feel it? Doesn't she get how what we have isn't normal? You don't just throw something like this away. She looks up at me, those beautiful chocolate eyes that hold my heart. When the song ends, we stand together as the next song starts before she tries to pull away. Is it because the song ended or is she trying to run away again?

I take her hand, and we walk off the dance floor together. Instead of taking us to our seats, I walk us out into the lobby. I don't let go of her hand.

"Sarah, what did you mean when you said Jessica was the reason you left?"

"I leave the day after tomorrow, Will. What's the point in even doing this?"

It feels like she slapped me. "What's the point? Sarah, you broke my heart when you left, and you tell Brian I don't get to hurt. I think I deserve to know what happened."

She snorts. "I broke your heart?" She sinks into a chair behind us.

I pull another chair around and sit so I'm facing her. I put my hands on her knees, and she puts her hands on mine.

14

She looks up at me. "Remember how the bugs kept biting me so I sat in your car while you were exchanging insurance info with Claire?"

That night, the night of our graduation, we went to a party at Bravo's. The plan was to spend the night. I finally worked up the nerve to ask her to come with me to school. She hadn't said yes, but I could tell she was thinking about it. Sometime during the night, we both start at a loud knock on our door. Claire Warner had backed into my car. Sarah went out with me while I went to see how bad it was and exchange insurance information. Sarah went to sit in my car because bugs kept biting her. That was the last time I saw her.

She takes a deep breath, spinning her ring "Jessica got in on the driver's side and told me about Italy, showed me a text *you* sent her."

I start shaking my head. "She lied. I didn't even know she was going until we got to the airport."

She glares at me. "She showed me a text from your number that said how happy you were she was going. That you made a mistake breaking up with her."

She tries to pull away from me, but I hold on to her. "Sarah, I never sent her a text, and I sure as shit did not regret breaking up with her. I didn't know her family was going to Italy until I saw them at the gate. I swear."

"Her family? She never said her family was going, and I saw the text and then she had me call the number from the text and you answered, and when I hung up, you called back."

"Yes, her mom, dad, and little brother. I have no clue what to tell you about the text. I know I didn't send it, and I don't remember a call that night, but I was freaking out about what my parents were going to do when they saw my car. If someone, anyone, called I probably answered, and if they hung up, I probably called them back."

We sit in silence looking at each other. I'm angry, thinking back to that night. When I couldn't find her, I freaked. Bravo had taken my keys away since I had been drinking that night. He even had to talk me out of checking the lake when I started to wonder if she had fallen in. Only after someone said they saw her leave with some girls was he able to get me back inside the house.

"Was there anything else?" I ask, my head swimming.

She closes her eyes.

"Please, tell me what happened," I plead.

"I need a drink, maybe two."

HER

"If I go get you a couple drinks will you still be here when I get back?"

She nods. For me it's a test. I can't do this anymore. I can't keep chasing her. It hurts too much. If she's gone when I come back with drinks, I'm leaving. I walk over to the bar and order four shots. Part of me expects her chair to be empty when I walk back into the hallway. Seeing her there, waiting for me, calms me. I pass her a shot glass. We lock eyes before throwing them back. She holds her hand out for the second, and I watch it drain into her mouth.

"Where did you go that night?" I ask, taking the glass and setting it with the others on a table behind my chair.

"Christie Howell and some other girl were leaving. I had my purse and got a ride home with them."

I drop my head into my hands. "I was losing my mind when I couldn't find you. I thought maybe someone had taken you or you had fallen into the lake or I don't know."

"I didn't think. I just had to get out of there."

"Why didn't you say something to me. I would have proved to you it wasn't true, whatever she said."

"I just never could believe you would want someone like me more than someone like her," she says, looking away.

How didn't she know, after everything we went through? My world began and ended with her. I can't understand how she could ever doubt the way I felt about her.

"Will?"

"I thought you knew how much I loved you." My throat feels thick. "How could you not know?"

"I didn't—I couldn't. You were the most popular guy in school. Every girl loved you. I still don't—"

"Stop." I hold up my hand. "Don't even go there. I didn't care about all of the stupid high school shit, and you knew that. You knew me. When I couldn't find you, I've never been more scared in my whole life. I must have called your phone a hundred times before I figured out it was in my car. I finally called Brian, and he told me you came home crying.

I almost drove over right then, but he told me to let you sleep and that we could talk in the morning. Bravo took my keys and wouldn't let me drive anywhere until the next morning because I was so freaked out. And then when I got to your house, you were gone." It hit me all over again, that day, not knowing where she was.

The ballroom door opens, filling the hallway with music. Her Uncle Chip comes walking out of the ballroom and over to us "You kids okay?"

I just look down.

"Are you sure?"

"We're just talking." She pauses. "It's okay."

Chip heads back into the ballroom, the hall filling once again with music until the door shuts.

She watches the door to the ballroom close. When her face turns back, our eyes lock.

"Seven years, Sarah. Did we really lose seven years because of a text?" I ask, stunned.

She shakes her head.

"Then why?"

The hall fills with music again when someone walks into the hall off in search of a restroom, most likely. She looks at me "Can we talk outside?"

I nod and stand, still holding her hand. We make our way to the front entrance, then follow a stone path along the left side of the building to a covered patio. There are ceiling fans slowly creating a slight breeze and black wrought iron tables and chairs. It's June. In Atlanta, the shade is welcome, but it's still humid. I let go of her hand and take off my jacket, draping over the back of a chair before pulling one out for her.

She waves me off. "I need to walk around if that's okay. You can sit, I just can't right this second."

I sit and watch her pace nervously back and forth in front of me. I snap. "Sarah, just tell me."

"I felt stupid the next morning for leaving the way I did. I wanted to call you but didn't know where my phone was." She starts spinning her ring.

"I can't believe I didn't even think to ask Brian for it, but I ended up calling your home phone."

I tilt my head at her, confused.

"I had to look up the number in the directory." She pauses. "Your mom answered."

This does not sound good.

"I asked for you, and she said you weren't home. I told her I couldn't find my phone and didn't know your number by heart."

The heels of her shoes click as she moves back and forth. She tried to call me. I never knew.

She glances over at me, still messing with her ring. "I asked her for your number or to let you know I called."

"She didn't tell me," I rasp.

She nods. "She said she wouldn't."

"Why?"

She looks down, slipping one of her feet out of her shoe and flexing her toes before slipping it back on and pacing again. "She told me I wasn't good enough for you. Then she told me Jessica was going with you to Italy."

"I told you I didn't know she was going," I argue.

"I believe you. It's just when I tried to argue with your mom, she said they wouldn't pay for your college if you were with me."

"Sarah, they didn't pay for my school at all."

Her mouth drops. "What?"

I rub my jaw. "My grandparents set up a trust when I was little. It paid for all of it and the apartment I planned to live in with my girlfriend." I say that last bit out of anger. God I thought she trusted me. I can't believe we wasted the last seven years because of stuff a simple conversation could have fixed.

"I didn't know."

I still can't figure out why my mom would do that. "She wouldn't. She—" I don't even realize I'm talking out loud until Sarah cuts me off.

She glares at me. "You believe whatever you want, Will. You asked why I left, and I told you."

She turns to go back inside. Not this time. I stand and grab her arm. She turns back to look at me, and I do exactly what I've waited all week to do.

My lips crush hers. Something about kissing Sarah feels like coming home, even though I never left. Her lips are the salvation I've been seeking for the last seven years. I thrill in tasting her again. From this point on, this girl is mine. She's right there with me. When we break our kiss, we each take a step back.

"You can't just kiss me."

Yes I can, and I will whenever the fuck I feel like it. "You didn't leave because you didn't love me?"

When she shakes her head, it hits me. I sink into a chair and drop my head into my hands. I don't know if she'll ever understand what her leaving did to me. She quietly sits down next to me. I'm trying to hold myself together, but I've missed her for so long.

She gasps and moves to wipe the threatening tears from my eyes. "I've loved you and only you, Sarah, for the last seven years. When you left, I never got over it."

"I didn't know. I thought I was doing the right thing. That you didn't love me as much as I loved you."

I take both of her hands in mine "Don't ever say that. Don't ever think that."

When her eyes start watering, I pull her into my lap. Our lips find each other. I care, but I don't care that we lost all of this together. None of that matters anymore. She is in my arms now. I can forgive the eighteen year old girl who was scared and ran away, as long as the woman in my arms today doesn't pull any stupid shit like that again.

We both turn our heads towards the sound of someone clearing their throat.

"Anything you two want to tell me?" Brian asks as he leans up against a post.

I pull her closer. "I'm in love with your little sister."

"Really?" Sarah asks.

I kiss the spot right below her ear. "Always."

"About fucking time," Brian laughs before heading back inside.

"But, you don't even know me anymore, and I don't know you. We can't just jump into something like this. I live in Denver. Seriously, what are we going to do?" she asks.

She wants me to prove it to her, fine. "I disagree, Sarah. I know you. I know your favorite sandwich. I know your favorite book. I know what you look like when you are sad and you don't want anyone to know. I know how much you loved your Grandma Bess, and I bet you still have her picture by your bed. I know where you're ticklish and that you love waffle cones. I know you hold your breath when you think your heart is racing and that you've done that every time I've been near you this week. Don't think that we're rushing or doing anything too fast, and about the other stuff, we'll figure it out. I want you to know that I will do anything to be with you."

She pulls back, putting her hands on my chest. "Will, you make it sound so easy, but I still have to leave. Do you want a long distance relationship?"

I don't think I can handle her leaving again. "Don't go."

She laughs. God, I love that sound. "Oh, it's that easy. What about my job?"

"I'm sure they'll get by without you for a while."

Her beautiful mouth drops. "Will, it's my company."

Shit, I hadn't expected that. "Like you own it?"

She nods, looking pretty damn proud of herself. She should be.

"You own a company?"

She shrugs "It's not a big company, but yes. It's mine, and this is the longest I've ever been away. I really do have to go back."

I pick up her hands and put them back around my neck. "I could come back with you. It is summer break."

"You would do that? Really?"

I'd follow her to the ends of the earth. I lean forward to kiss her. "I'm not letting you get away from me again."

"What about your mom?"

That right there. My mom is the fucking reason she left, the reason we've been apart for the last seven years, and she's worried about her. That is one of the reasons she is the only girl for me. "I've done all I can for her. I'm not even sure she'd notice if I left."

"Don't say that."

"It's true. I hate to say it, but she hasn't been right since Bethany's death. I don't know why she said what she said to you, but I believe you. I'm so sorry she did that, that Jessica did that. Please know that you have always been all I've ever wanted."

When my lips find her neck, she asks. "Should we head back inside?"

"Nope, don't want to." I'm not sure I'll ever let her go.

"William."

I know she thinks I hate it when she calls me that. I look up and smirk before releasing her waist. I pine the loss of her body the moment she stands up. I watch her for a moment, fixing her dress. I've always heard girls complain about bridesmaid dresses, but Sarah looks gorgeous. I stand and swing my jacket over one shoulder and reach for her hand.

I can't help it. As we walk off the patio, I glance down at her. "Just think if you would have talked to me the first day you got back."

I grunt when she elbows me. I deserve it, even though it's true.

Once we're back in the ballroom, I drop my jacket off at our table and pull her out to the edge of the dance floor. "I think you owe me a dance, Miller Lite."

As we make our way onto the dance floor, Sarah stops and puts her hand on her chest when the next song starts. I look at her, confused, until I hear the lyrics. Kind of meant to be that we'd dance to a song about being in love with your best friend. The dance floor is all ours. Most of our friends and family here know our history. I'm still not expecting them to clap at the end of the song. I hope the attention isn't embarrassing her, so I kiss her forehead as Brian and Christine come over to hug us.

Sarah blushes. "Guys, this is your day. Please don't make a big deal about this."

"Me make a big deal?" Brian hams as he walks over to the DJ and borrows his mic. "Hey, everyone. Let's give a hand to one of my best friends, Will, and my baby sister, Sarah. Will has only been in love with her forever, and it only took like a decade for him to seal the deal. To Sarah and Will."

"To Sarah and Will," everyone exclaims, raising their glasses.

She buries her head in my chest. I lift her chin and softly kiss her as everyone around us cheers. The rest of the evening, we are almost as popular as Brian and Christine. First, her mom and dad came over to gush about how they always knew we would end up together and now this means she'll be moving back home. I'm trying not to laugh at her as she bites her lips and sweetly nods at every crazy thing that comes out of her mother's mouth. When she brings up children, her father pulls her away after Sarah shoots him a pointed look.

Sarah raises her glass. "Well, that wasn't awkward, was it?"

I don't get why she's nervous. I'm a sure thing. I know now nothing has felt right for the last seven years. Like trying to walk with a rock in your shoe. You can do it, and sometimes the rock moves out of the way up against the edge of your shoe so you don't really notice it until it shifts again. But you don't truly feel relief until it's gone. That's how I feel, like a weight has been lifted and I can just enjoy life again. I know there's shit we'll have to figure out, and it will probably suck at some point now or in the future.

I can't stop touching her, even when we aren't dancing my hand is searching for her skin to warm it. We follow everyone out to wave off Brian and Christine. They've booked a swanky hotel room for tonight and will leave for their honeymoon tomorrow.

Once they pull out of sight, I look at her. "Want to get out of here? We can get a room."

"Um, I..." she stammers.

Shit. I don't want to scare her off. I tug her into my arms and murmur. "We don't have to do anything." I mean it. I'm just not ready for tonight to end. I want to talk to her and hold her and fall asleep next to her.

"What if we lay down some ground rules?" she suggests.

I hate rules. "What kind of rules?"

"No sex."

Ever? Or just tonight? Might as well be honest. "Not sure I can agree to that one."

"Will, I just don't think we should rush."

Last thing I want is for her to feel rushed. Ever. I can be Wesley to her Buttercup forever as long as she doesn't leave me again. "As you wish."

She smiles, but I can tell she's not buying it. "Could we go somewhere and talk?"

Go somewhere? Done. I take her hand and lead her over to her parents. "Mr. and Mrs. Miller, I'm kidnapping your daughter."

They don't seem surprised. Now I need to figure out where to go. I'm pretty sure a hotel room will freak her out, and there's no way I'm bringing her back to my house. Her house is out too since her parents and Uncle Chip are going to be there. As we drive to her house, I reach out and put my hand on her leg. I wait to see if she's going to say something or push it off. When she doesn't, I relax and think of the perfect place, Brian's house. At a red light, I text him to see if it's cool. His reply? *Do NOT have sex with my little sister in my house.* I don't reply.

This is one hundred percent Sarah's show. If all she wants to do is talk, that's all we're doing. I have a spare key to Brian's place. We swing by her parents' place first for Sarah to change and grab some stuff. I follow her upstairs. I don't want to be away from her. There's a part of me that doesn't accept that this is actually happening. She tosses some things into a small bag and walks into the bathroom; I can't help it. I follow her. She starts taking these little metal sticks out of her hair. There seem to be hundreds of them.

I move over to help her. Her hair smells like pears, and I inhale, stopping myself from burying my face in her hair. Her eyes open and find mine. When she left, I had been the only guy she had ever been with. I don't want to know, but I can't stop myself. "Sarah, has there been anyone since me, you know, for you."

"In what way?"

I gnaw on my lip. "Sexually."

"Have I had sex since you?"

Why did I even ask? I drop my head and nod.

"Yes, I've had relationships over the last seven years, Will." I'm assaulted with images in my head of other guys touching her. She pauses. "Have you?"

I look up. I'm not proud about it, but I nod.

"So neither of us has anything to be worried about, right? Just…" She gets a weird look on her face, like she's in pain. "Did you get back together with Jessica after I left?"

What? "No way."

I grab one of her hands and kiss it. With each pin I take out, her hair loosens and tumbles into my hands. I drag my fingers across her scalp, watching her eyes flutter closed. She leans back against me, at first stiffly, but after a moment, I feel her soften and relax into me. It's like every moment with her is more right than the moment before it. When her eyes open, I see want in them; I keep my eyes on her, and I push her hair out of the way and kiss her neck. She sags into me for just a moment before she leans forward, gripping the counter.

"You stay here or go downstairs. I'm going to change out of my dress."

I can't help it. "You sure you don't need help with that?"

She points downstairs, and I go, giving her my best pout before I piss her off.

She doesn't take long and is talking to someone as she walks down the stairs. I freeze when I hear her say I love you before she hangs up.

I suck at nonchalance. "Who do you love?"

She tucks her phone into the back pocket of some extremely tight jeans. "Spy much?"

I shrug.

She walks over to me and wraps her arms around my waist. "It was Sawyer, my new best friend."

Fuck. I don't even know him, and I think I hate him.

She looks up at me. "What's wrong?"

Be nice. "What's he like?"

She laughs at me. "Will, Sawyer is a girl. All better now?"

I'm a dumbass.

She calls me on it. "You were jealous."

Hell yeah, I was jealous. I see her looking up at me, her smile an invitation my lips can't resist. I claim her mouth, my tongue the flag marking her mine. I kiss her until my message is given loud and clear. When I lift my head, she looks good and dazed. "Yes, I was jealous. I just happen to know your last best friend fell in love with you so I got nervous."

15

I'm alone with Sarah. Alone, alone. We've been alone, like just now at her parents' house, but we both knew they were coming home and could walk in at any moment. This is different, she has an overnight bag. I don't care if she even lets me kiss her again tonight. I'm waking up tomorrow in the same place she is.

She needs to know that's how I hope to spend every morning from here on out, waking up where she is. After I park, I look over at her. She opens her mouth, and I just know she's going to say we're rushing things or it'll never work or the distance will be an issue. I don't care. I already know it will be hard. I don't need her psyching herself out.

I lean over and kiss her, lifting my lips to tell her to shut up between each kiss.

I'm trying to be cute, playful. She bites my bottom lip, and I have to stop myself from hauling her into my lap and showing her just how bad I want her.

She knows she's starting something. She watches me as she let's go of my lip.

I don't want to scare her off. I take a deep breath. "I've been dreaming about having you in my arms again for seven years, Sarah."

She gulps, blinking away the wetness from her eyes that make them shine from the light of the streetlamp before mouthing 'me too.' I get out and grab her bag before walking around and opening her door.

I feel the silence. "Did you know I used to live here?" I ask, taking her hand in mine.

"Christine told me. She pointed out your old place from their balcony. Said something about you and Brian trying to play catch between both places."

I laugh. God, that feels like a long time ago. "It was fun living here. I miss that place."

My thumb rests on the inside of her wrist, and I can feel her pulse racing against it. I look at her reflection in the mirrored doors of the elevator, Sarah holding her breath. I lean over and kiss her neck, right below her ear just to feel her pulse flutter against my lips.

"Remember that thing I said about you holding your breath when you think your heart is pounding?" Her eyes lock on mine. "You're doing it right now," I breathe into her ear.

We both look up at the sound of the elevator's arrival. As soon as we're inside, I close the space between us, I need her lips on mine. I need her arms under my neck as mine coil around her waist pulling her closer to me. I don't stop until we get to Brian's floor.

She pushes off of me. "Remember, we're just talking tonight."

I chew on the corner of my lip. She might act innocent, but she wasn't stopping that kiss in the elevator.

Once we're inside, I ask, "Want a drink, Miller Lite?"

She laughs. "No one has called me that in…"

I lift my hand to cup her beautiful face. "Seven years?"

She nods as I lower my lips to hers once again. This kiss is different from the intensity of the one in the elevator. This one has a trace of sadness to it, the pain of time we lost together of all those years.

She breaks our kiss. "Will, we need to talk."

I'm not done with her yet. I nip and kiss across her jaw. "This is more fun."

"Will, I leave the day after tomorrow." My mood sinks just thinking about it.

I tug her earlobe between my teeth and lick the edge of it before stepping back. "Drink?"

"Just water."

I go in the kitchen, pour her some water and grab a beer for myself. When I walk back into the living room, I make a face when I see where she's sitting. She picked the armchair over the sofa. I'm tempted to scoop her up and make her sit in my lap, but I'm not sure how pissed that will make her. I hand her the glass of water, purposefully brushing my fingers across hers. I have seven years worth of touching her to get out of my system.

I set my beer on the coffee table and tug off my bow tie. I had planned on just unbuttoning the top button of my shirt but decide to take it off when I catch Sarah watching me. By the time I have my dress shirt off and hanging over the side of the armchair, she's blushing. I'm still wearing an undershirt. I sit on the sofa and take a drink of my beer.

I wait until she's had a chance to recover. "Alright, Sarah. Let's talk."

"I'm scared, Will. This whole thing scares me. I have no idea what we're doing, and it's all happening so fast, and then there's the fact that I live in Colorado and you live here and you have your hands full with your mom. You have to know I'm a planner. This not knowing what is going to happen is not something I'm good at."

I chew on the side of my lip while she talks. She's scared, and it kills me. I need to hold her. I need to convince her that none of that other stuff matters as long as we're together. I do what I've wanted to do since the second I saw her sitting in that armchair. I scoop her up into my arms, holding her tight as she tries to wiggle away and sit back down with her in my lap.

"I'm scared too, Sarah, but I know that this is going to work out. You and I are going to happen.

There isn't anyone else for me. I'm not going to let you run again. I'm not. Things might suck for a bit while we figure all the details out, but we can't let that stop us from being together. Did you ever think we would have a normal relationship? Does that even exist? Our feelings are as real as it gets. When I kiss you it's real, and I know you feel it too. I feel like I've been sleep walking for the last seven years and then I saw you on the plane, and it was like I was awake again."

She melts into me, and I relax further against the back of the sofa, her body following mine.

I ask her about her company, about moving back here. If it isn't possible, I want her to know I'll move. I'll leave everything here to be with her. I wait, gently dragging my fingertips up and down her back as she thinks about it. I'm just happy she hasn't made a move to get off of my lap. She starts talking leases and head counts and if they all go remote maybe it could work this way or another way. I barely hear the details. I'm too focused on the fact that it sounds like we can do this, that, maybe not this month, but soon, she could move back here.

If she's willing to figure all of that out, I need to do the same with my mom. "It'd mean a lot to me if you would come over tomorrow and talk to my mom with me." I feel her tense in my arms. "Please, Sarah."

"I'm not sure that's a good idea, Will."

I'm pissed at what my mom did all those years ago. I can never take back what she said to Sarah. I also know that after my dad's death, she caved more into herself. She isn't that person anymore. I hate what she did, but she will always be my mom.

"If you want me to, I'll go," she finally says.

God, I love her. I tighten my arms around her. "If I want you to? Does that hold for everything?" My lips are against her ear.

She laughs. "You are impossible."

I'm sick of talking. "Haven't we talked enough?" I mumble against the skin of her neck.

"Will."

I ignore her. "Will!"

I still ignore her. "WILL!"

Man, she's loud. "Yes, dear."

"We're not going to do stuff on my brother's couch."

If location is the issue, I can fix that. She gasps as I stand with her still in my arms. "S'cool. They have a spare bedroom."

I ignore her grumbles as I carry her there, using my foot to kick the door closed behind us and my elbow to flip on the light. I set her on the edge of the bed, kneeling in front of her. I plan on worshiping her if she'll let me. I kiss her, gently nibbling on her lip. I'm almost lost in the taste of her when she starts giggling. What's so funny? I pull back and look at her, arching a brow.

She shrugs, still giggling "Sorry, you're just always biting your lip. Now mine too?"

She's cute when she makes fun of me. "Kind of kills my trying to seduce you when you laugh at me."

"Oh, that's what's happening here?"

All right, she just asked for it. I grab her by the waist and pull her onto the floor. She's on her back, eyes wide as she stares up at me. Before, I wanted to worship her. Now I want to dominate her. She might own her own company and be the boss, but if I have my way, she'll be screaming my name in a little while. Her giggles are now moans as she bucks against me, her hands reaching down to pull me closer to her. When they move up to grip my shoulders, I lean back and grab them, pinning them over her head.

Sarah looks up at me panting. I take it she likes that. I drop my lips back to hers as I hold her hands above her head in one hand as I crawl my other hand up the inside of her shirt to cup and squeeze her breast. She gasps against my mouth, and I pull back to make sure it was a good one. When she arches her back, pushing herself against my hand, I lick my lips thinking about what I'm going to do to her.

She pulls her hands from my grasp and tugs at my shirt. I sit back, tugging it forward over my head. I'm about to lie back down on her when she scrambles up, mouth open to look at my tattoo, *her* tattoo.

"When?" she asks, her fingers brushing over it.

"'Bout seven years ago," I admit.

I freeze as I watch her lean down and kiss it, the warmth of her lips on my chest. I always wondered how she would react if she ever saw it. This has to be better than anything I could have imagined. I need her, all of her, so bad. I drag her face up to mine and crush my lips to hers. She stops me as I lower her back down to the ground. I pull back. Are we going to fast? I don't want to stop, but I don't want her to freak out either. I exhale as I watch her pull off her shirt. She lies down, and I'm at a loss at where to start. I kiss her stomach and smile as her muscles flex beneath my lips. I kiss my way up her side and chuckle against her skin when I hit a spot where she's ticklish and she starts wiggling.

Her breasts are calling out to me, though, and I can't ignore them. I bury my face in her cleavage and kiss and lick every inch of them not covered by her bra. She arches her back and reaches behind herself to unhook her bra. Using both hands, I drag the straps down her arms. With one hand I cup one breast, rolling my thumb over the hardened tip. My lips are on her other breast, sucking her into my mouth, circling her with my tongue. Her hands are in my hair, her nails on my scalp as she pulls me closer. I know what she wants, but I'm just waiting for her to ask. I keep my hand on her breast and kiss my way to her neck.

"Will, kiss me," she pleads.

I take her mouth, my tongue working her over, and pick her up, leaning her against the back of the bed. I love her lips, but I can't ignore her beautiful breasts. Her head falls back onto the bed as I touch, kiss, and nip at them. I want her so bad. I lower my hand to the button of her jeans, and she stills.

"Is this okay?"

She says something that sounds like yes, but I ask again just to be sure. She pushes my hand away and unbuttons them herself. I lift her up, setting her on the edge of the bed. She falls back, and I pull off her shoes.

"You're going to wanna hold on," I say, lowering the fly of her jeans and sliding them down her legs. I rest my hands on the edge of her panties. It's a question. If she wants me to go any further, she knows how to answer. She does, lifting her hips. I ease them down her legs and drop them. She tries to hide herself from me. Not happening. I grab her behind her knees and pull them apart and drag her closer to the edge of the bed.

I kiss my way up her thighs. "You have no idea how long I've wanted to do this again."

With her hands in my hair, I consume her. I lick, suck, nip, and kiss her until she falls apart. I've fantasized about having her in my arms again for the last seven years. The fantasy is nothing in comparison to the real thing, but it kept me going all these years. I lift my head to give her a cocky you're welcome when I see the tears running down her face. I move to her, pulling her into my arms and wipe the tears from her eyes. She sobs against my chest as I stroke her hair. Her breathing evens out, and I see she's asleep. I shift the blanket and sheet from under us to cover her. I walk back into the living room and finish my beer in one gulp.

I know she's hurting, but I'm going to do everything I can to help her. I walk back in the spare room and take off my pants before sliding into bed with her. I reach for her, wrapping her in my arms.

I wake to Sarah trying to pull away from me. I tighten my arms around her "You're not getting away this time, Sarah"

"Aww, that's sweet and all, but unless you're into golden showers, you're going to wanna let me go to the bathroom."

I'm a dick. I squeeze her tighter.

"Will, if you make me pee in my big brother's bed, I will never forgive you."

"Where's the romance?" I release her.

"That kind of romance is only in movies, where people never use the bathroom or have morning breath," she shouts as I watch her naked ass dash out of the room.

I get up and use the bathroom in Brian and Christine's room. I think about what she said about morning breath and grab my toothbrush and toothpaste on my way into the kitchen. She laughs when she sees me brushing my teeth. I shrug, and she comes up behind me and wraps her arms around my waist. She's got a towel wrapped around her. I rinse my mouth and turn to kiss her, pleasantly surprised she already brushed her teeth too. I pull off her towel and set her on their island.

"This can't be sanitary," she laughs.

I stand between her legs and pause when her hands move to my boxers. I'm trying to respect the whole no sex rule, minus oral, but she doesn't seem to mind that.

"I want you inside me."

There is nowhere I would rather be. Shit. "I don't have any condoms."

"I have an implant."

That's a new one. "Do what?" I pull back and look at her.

"It's birth control implanted in my arm," She points to a slight raised line on her arm. I peer at it.

"Why?"

"Don't laugh?"

This should be good. I lift a brow.

"Okay, so Sawyer, my best friend, is very much a free spirit. She could never remember to take the pill and had a couple of pregnancy scares. She needed a more long term solution but was too scared to do it by herself, so being a good friend and not wanting to ever have to read another pregnancy exam to her ever, I agreed to get one so she wouldn't be alone."

That means we can...right now. "So what you're saying," I move my hand between her thighs, "is we can be very spontaneous?"

She nods and that's all the answer I need. My mouth finds her, and I carry her back into the spare room, her legs wrapped around my waist. I lay her down, covering her, grinding against her, before I stand to lose my boxers.

Her eyes blink open.

"Are you sure?" I ask.

She nods, reaching out for me.

Nope, not good enough. "I want to hear you say it."

She groans, lifting my chin until our eyes are level. "Yes, I'm sure."

My lips cut her off as I sink into her. She's wet and tight and feels like heaven on earth. I stop kissing her only to watch her, to see her face as she moves beneath me, against me, and with me. I've never seen anything more beautiful. I've never really realized until this moment just how much I missed her. There is nothing sexier than the sound of my name on her lips. I feel her build up, and I know I'm close. I lean down to kiss her and groan as I go. I can't stop kissing her. I scatter them all over the side of her face.

She giggles. "Will, we just did it."

I can't help it. "God, I love you."

I watch her face fall before she tries to hide it against my chest.

I gently lift her chin. "Sarah, what's wrong?"

Helplessly, I watch her shake her head even though I see the tears in her tears. "Please tell me."

She closes her eyes and sniffles as she speaks. "I'm so sorry I left. I'm so sorry I did that to you. Please believe me."

I put my hands on both sides of her face and kiss her. "Don't cry. I love you." I give her another kiss. "Please don't cry. I would do anything for you." I give her another kiss. "Please look at me."

I blink away tears of my own and give her another kiss. "We were so young." Another kiss. Her eyes open. "You didn't know." Another kiss. "We can't change the past." Another kiss. "We're together now." Another kiss. "I just want to make you happy."

I'm scared I've said the wrong thing when she starts to cry even more until she pulls my lips to hers. "I love you so much." Another kiss. "You make me happier than I have ever been." Another kiss. "Why are you crying?"

"I don't know. I feel like an emotional wreck. Are you sure you want all of this?"

I'd marry her tomorrow. "There is nothing I have ever wanted more."

16

We pull up in front of my house. I can tell she's nervous. She's been spinning her ring the whole drive over here. I lean over to kiss her, hoping this isn't a bad idea. Part of me wants to be back at Brian and Christine's getting reacquainted. Her hand is in mine when we walk in. I'm relieved when I see my mom in the living room, looking fairly normal.

"Hi, Mom."

She turns to look at us but doesn't say anything. I notice her eyes move to our linked hands before looking back up at Sarah. Sarah and I walk further into the room and sit on the sofa.

"Mom." She looks over at me. "Do you remember my friend, Sarah Miller?"

She looks at Sarah again and then at our still joined hands. She nods.

I take a breath. "Sarah lives in Colorado now, and since I'm on summer break, I'd like to go out and visit her. Do you think that would be alright?"

She doesn't do anything immediately, but after a moment, her face crumbles and she lifts her hands to cover her face. Shit. That did not go well. I let go of Sarah's hand and go over to her.

"It's okay, Mom. Shhh. There's no reason to be upset." I try and calm her down, rubbing her back. She leans into me, gripping my shoulders as she cries. I glance over at Sarah, who looks uncomfortable as hell. Once I finally get my mom calm, I go upstairs with Sarah so I can change. No way I'm leaving the two of them alone. Sarah is tense. I tug her into my arms once we're in my room.

"Have you left her by herself before?"

I gnaw on my lip. "Nothing longer than a night here and there since my dad died."

"She just doesn't leave the house?"

"Not since she came back from the hospital that day."

Her brows crease. "But she takes care of herself otherwise?"

"She doesn't cook anymore but will eat things that are already prepared. I keep the kitchen stocked with ready made stuff."

"What do you want to do?"

What can I do? "Ideally, maybe hire someone to stay with her while I'm gone." I should have done that a long time ago.

She frowns. "Do you know anyone?"

I shake my head. I've seen those caregiver commercials on TV. I guess I'd need to call them and get some referrals, maybe interview some people. What if they couldn't start right away? I look at Sarah and wonder if she's reading my mind.

It might be harder than I thought it would be for me to follow her out to Colorado.

I change, grinning to myself when I catch Sarah checking me out. "I'm going to go check on her again. I'll be right back." I lean down to give her another kiss before I go.

I head to the kitchen first to see if there are any plates in the sink. That's the only way I can tell if she's eaten anything or not. There's a bowl with some oatmeal left in it, I rinse it and put it in the dishwasher. I know she probably isn't too hungry since she's upset, so I make her a light lunch of some cheese and crackers with fruit on the side. I have no idea if she'll eat it, but I feel better doing it. She's still sitting in the same chair in the living room. I kiss the top of her head and set the plate down on the table next to her and head back upstairs.

Sarah's on her phone when I walk in.

"Hang on a sec, Sawyer." She rests her phone on her shoulder. "Will, Sawyer offered to come stay with your mom."

What? I reach out my hand. "Can I talk to her?"

After she tells Sawyer, she passes me the phone. "Hi, Sawyer."

"Hey, stud. Want me to come mamasit?"

I glance over at Sarah. If it means getting to be with her. "Maybe, have you ever done anything like this before?"

"Mamasit? Nope, this would be a first, but I'm good with people and Sarah said she showers and dresses herself. Right? She does shower and dress herself?"

"Yes, she does shower and dress herself." I look down. "But she has days where she doesn't from time to time. It's been a really long time since there have been two days like that in a row."

"But it could happen?"

"Yes, and I'm not sure if her behavior might be erratic if I leave just because of change."

There's a pause. "Has she ever been violent?"

I shake my head. "No, just cries a lot and refuses to leave the house."

"I can handle that, and if it ever gets to the point where I can't, I can call you."

"Are you sure about this?" I glance over at Sarah and hope her answer is yes.

"Will, I met Sarah the day she left Georgia, *the day*. I have known her for seven years and love her more than anyone else I can think of off the top of my head. She has never sounded happier, talking about you. I would love to mamasit for you."

We talk for another couple of minutes as Sawyer checks flight schedules. She already knows Sarah's flight information because she was planning on picking her up from the airport. Now she's looking for the next flight to Atlanta and trying to get me a seat on Sarah's flight to Denver. I ask if she wants to talk to Sarah. She says no, letting me know she just booked a flight and expects our asses to come pick her up around midnight.

I hang up and jump on her to give her the good news, which we find leads to some very fun, half clothed celebration sex. I'm loving her implant thing. I somehow manage to pack, even though I find her utterly distracting. She waits in my car while I go talk to my mom again and let her know Sawyer will be coming to stay with her a while. I'm not even sure she hears me. If her eyes weren't open and blinking, she could have been asleep. This gives me no idea of how the introduction will go.

We spend the rest of the day at her house, with her parents and uncle Chip. Mr. and Mrs. M are thrilled, Chip less so. He doesn't know me the way they do. I know he's just looking out for Sarah. He's the one who picked up the pieces the last time around. I glance at her, watch her tuck a strand of chestnut hair behind her ear. Sometime over the week, my feelings for her had evolved. When it started, she was this fantasy, the answer to what had plagued me the last seven years. She was also a giant pain in my ass, and I loved her for that, for still being the girl I fell in love with all those years ago. Now she also has this poise, this confidence in the way she talks to her parents or about her business.

I'm looking forward to seeing more of that side of her, the career woman. The things she organizes for small businesses and their employees' sounds really confusing. I'm so impressed by her and so conscious of how alive she makes me feel. Her parents have already gotten an email from the newlyweds. They made it to Turks and Cacaos and wanted to thank everyone again for making their day so special. Mrs. M has nothing but future grandbabies on the mind. Chip tells her to shut up after she mentions Sarah and I will probably make beautiful babies.

I silently thank the maker of the implant thing in Sarah's arm. I don't know if she even wants kids someday, but for now, I really don't want to share her with anyone. After dinner, we watch movies until it's time to go pick up Sawyer from the airport.

In the car, I ask her to tell me more about her. It's weird to think I'm going to let someone I've never met keep an eye on my mom. I go back and forth between feeling like a shitty son to not knowing what else I can do for her. Because I'm her son, because I know her history, do I enable her to dwell in this never-ending cycle of grief?

Sarah's quiet on the way to the airport. I squeeze her leg. "Are you doing okay?"

An evening storm had broken the humidity that seemed to always hover this time of year. It's almost chilly without it. She pulls her black sweater tighter around herself and looks at me. "You're coming home with me tomorrow."

I agree. "I am."

A sleepy smile breaks across her face. "I still can't believe it."

I can't either. I think I'll wake up scared that this has all been a vivid dream.

She keeps going. "It will feel more real when Sawyer meets you."

I groan. "Am I going to have to pass some secret test?"

She laughs. "No, no test. You're in."

When we get to the airport, we have to go from the arrival gate straight to baggage claim when we see her flight landed early. One minute, I'm holding Sarah's hand, the next she's running full speed to a girl with pink hair. Pink hair? My mom is going to flip and not in a good way. I walk over to them and hold out my hand to someone I can only assume is Sawyer.

She pushes it away and hugs me instead. She's short so she's hugging my waist. I pat her back as I chew on the side of my lip. When I look away, Sarah starts laughing. My eyes flick to hers, and she sticks her tongue out at me. I am in charge of luggage and follow them to my car. It feels good when I hear Sawyer tell her she's never seen her look this happy. I did that, me. The ride to my house gets awkward when she asks why I didn't follow Sarah to New Jersey.

"I did."

Sarah's mouth drops. "What?"

"I was a wreck after you left. My dad almost canceled the trip to Italy, but my mom talked him out of it. I barely remember the trip. I was in this fog of worrying about what happened to you. You just disappeared and Brian wouldn't tell me right away where you went. I didn't even know you went to your uncle's until after I got back. The day I found out, I drove up there. I had to stop and stay in a shitty motel on the way 'cause there was construction happening on some bridge and it took forever to get over it.

I just couldn't wait to see you, to hold you, to bring you back with me. I didn't know why you left, but I knew I could get you to come back. When I got to your uncle's place, no one was home. I just sat in my car and waited for like two hours. I was just thinking about driving to get some food when I saw you pull up with some guy in a truck." I pause, trying not to think about how it felt to see her with someone else. "You were laughing. You both got out of the truck and walked around to the back to take out a giant stuffed monkey."

Sawyer gasps, and I stop.

Sarah looks at me, putting her hand on my leg. "Jake and I were never together, Will. I was helping him find a silly present for Sawyer that day. He was her boyfriend at the time."

"I still have that monkey," Sawyer grumbles from the back seat.

That means, all this time… "When I saw you together, how happy you looked. I thought, I just figured you had moved on."

She shakes her head.

"She never moved on," Sawyer adds from the back seat.

"Sawyer!"

"What? It's the truth. You buried yourself in school and then your business, half-heartedly dated when I forced you to, but you never moved on."

I park in front of my house and take her face in my hands. "I never moved on either."

I lean forward and kiss her, not stopping until we hear Sawyer clear her throat from the backseat.

"Will."

I meet her eyes through the rear view mirror. "Yeah."

"I know people. You ever, even unintentionally hurt Sarah and there will be no place you can hide from me."

Sarah flips around to face her. "Holy shit, Sawyer."

I think she's growing on me. "Thank you for taking care of my girl. All I plan to do is spend the rest of my life making her smile."

Sawyer looks at her. "Okay, I approve."

They wait outside while I take her bags in. My mom is already asleep. I really hope she doesn't freak out on Sawyer tomorrow. I double check the fridge, a list of important numbers and the spare room before I go back outside. Sarah and Sawyer hug again, and I give her my keys. Mr. and Mrs. M are going to drive my car back over tomorrow so Sawyer can use it while she's helping out with my mom.

Mrs. M promised to check in on her and show her where stuff was around town. Sarah isn't too worried. Sawyer used to do a lot of traveling and didn't always have a plan when she got places. She was flexible like that.

We crash when we get to her parents' house. I vaguely remember her taking off her clothes in front of me but figure that was a dream. I do remember her being a punk brat after her shower. I spend most of mine plotting my revenge. When I go downstairs for breakfast. I head outside to their back deck to call Sawyer first.

She answers right away. "Whadup?"

"Hi, Sawyer. It's Will. Just calling to see how the morning went."

"So your mom breaks out Italian when she's pissed?"

She does? "Other than that trip to Italy, I haven't heard her speak Italian unless she's on the phone, but she doesn't talk on the phone that much. Why what happened?"

"I'm the pink devil, which between you and me, might just be the coolest thing someone has ever called me in another language. I'm thinking of having t-shirts made."

"I'm confused. So she called you that in Italian?" I scratch the back of my neck.

"Yes, that and a, well, I'm actually not going to say the other thing. I'm kinda surprised at her." I hear her cover the phone and say something off to the side. "Aren't you lucky I'm not telling Will what you said? Might make him blush."

Now I don't know if I want to know what my mom is saying or not.

Sawyer returns to talking to me. "Either way, don't you worry about us. I'm sure we're going to be braiding each other's hair in no time, right potty mouth?"

My mom must be sitting near her because I know that last part wasn't for me. She just called my mother a potty mouth, to her face. That's the funniest thing I've ever heard.

Sarah sees me laughing as I walk back in. "What happened?"

"I didn't know your friend spoke Italian. I feel bad for laughing, but after my mom called her a bunch of names thinking she wouldn't understand, Sawyer told her off. In Italian." I shake my head. "Man, I wish I saw it."

"Are they going to be okay? That doesn't seem like a good start," her mom asks.

"Nah, they'll be fine. I think Sawyer might be just what my mom needs."

We hang out with the family until it's time to head to the airport. Mrs. M takes us, giving me an extra squeeze before we leave and making me promise to bring her girl home. Sarah does a double take when we print our boarding passes and she sees we're now sitting in first class. When Sawyer booked my ticket she couldn't swing two seats next to each other in coach so she upgraded Sarah's seat and bought me the one next to it.

I glance over at Sarah as she fastens her lap belt. Our reconnection, our second chance, all started on a plane less than a week ago. Turning around to see the girl who haunted me the last seven years was the last thing I ever expected, and now to be going home with her is crazy.

The flight is direct. We could have watched a show or a movie, but instead we just hold hands and talk. Sarah talks a lot about her job. She's nervous, but it helps her to be able to go through the possible scenarios out loud. Somehow it calms her, talking about it to me. I run my thumb back and forth across the top of her hand. Can't lie, I don't understand everything she is saying, but I'm riveted. She could read the phone book to me, and I'd still be hooked. She just looks at me with her beautiful, expressive chocolate eyes. You can tell she loves what she does, and it's infectious.

After we land and have our bags, she leads the way to the parking deck. I have a laugh when I see Sawyer's car. Little, pink-haired Sawyer drives a Hummer. If she was a dude, I'd wonder if she was compensating. I hitch a brow at Sarah.

She shrugs. "She figures if she gets in an accident, she'll just drive over the other car."

"What is her deal?" I ask, putting our bags in the back.

"She never told me the whole story, but she doesn't seem to worry about money. It's not something she ever talks about."

It's a trip, watching Sarah drive this big ass Hummer. Can't lie, it's kinda hot. She points out stuff along the way. I'm doing my best to avoid her noticing my attention is mainly on her legs. When we get to her condo, she takes the smaller, carryon bags and carries them up the flight of stairs that leads to her front door. I don't even notice the weight of our checked bags. My eyes are locked on her ass. Once we're in, the bags are piled off to the side, and I pin her to the back of the door, my lips on her neck.

"Well, hello," she sighs.

"Hey." My hands move to the hem of her dress.

"I have a bed, you know."

"Here's good," I say, unbuttoning my shorts.

Her eyes glaze over. I push the fabric of her panties to the side and lift her onto me. Her legs wrap around my waist, her hands on my shoulders. We're nose to nose, eyes locked as I pump in and out of her. Her mouth drops open, and as much as I want to kiss her, I don't want to stop looking at her. She is so beautiful. Like liquid, she floats over me and fills my every imperfection. To watch her, really watch her, when I'm inside her makes me feel invincible.

When her nails dig into my shoulders and her breath comes out in little pants, I know she's close. Her eyes melt into mine. I tighten my grip on her and buck into her. I feel crazy, needing her like this and partly stupid for not taking her to bed and savoring every inch of her. There's time for that. Right now, though, I need her fast and hard. She throws her head back and bangs it on the door. I have a split second of wondering if that hurt before the way her body tightens around me sends me crashing over as well.

After a moment of just looking at each other as we catch our breath, I shift her weight and reach up to rub the back of her head. "How's your head?"

She blushes. "Shut up."

I laugh and nip at her bottom lip. "I'm being serious. That sounded like it hurt."

She lifts one hand from my shoulders and gingerly touches her head a couple inches below where my hand is. "I barely felt it at the time. Hurts a little now, though," she admits.

I turn around, moving my hands to grip her as I walk her over to the sofa. I ease out of her as I lower her to the cushions and reach down to fix her clothes. "You sit, doctor's orders," I joke when she tries to get up.

Her kitchen opens onto the living room. I fix my shorts on the way and dig around her freezer and find an icepack. By the time I get back to her, she's lying on her back, a pillow under her head. I slip my hand under her neck and lift her head enough to slip the ice pack under it.

"Is this necessary?" she pouts.

I lean down and kiss her, taking my time, pulling back only when I taste her desire to argue disappear. "Yes, ma'am. I need you all healed up for what I'm planning on doing to you tonight."

Her mouth drops, and she nods. The living room has a big picture window with a decent view of some far off mountains. Her place is simple but comfortable. It feels lived in.

I walk back over to our bags. "Which way is your room?"

She points to the left. I have our big bags. I pass a half bath before I get to her room. It's a good size. She has a queen sized bed with a black and white printed comforter and a padded green headboard. That'll come in handy; I laugh to myself thinking of Sarah and her icepack on the sofa. There are nightstands on either side of the bed. One clearly more used than the other. I set my bags on the side opposite of it.

She has a full bath, with a soaker tub off her room. I make a mental note of the things we can do in that tub before going back to check on her. I smirk when I see she has her phone.

"I only got up for a minute," she blushes.

"I could've gotten it for you," I say, picking up her feet and setting them in my lap as I sit down.

"I just wanted to text everyone that we made it safe and sound. No head wounds mentioned."

I chew on the corner of my lip and reach out to stroke her arm. "How does it feel?"

"Cold," she giggles.

I make a face, and she sticks out her tongue, lifting her head and pulling the ice pack off the pillow. "I don't think I really need this."

I move her legs and stand up, leaning over to kiss her as I take the pack from her. "Can I get you something from the kitchen?" I ask over my shoulder as I walk to the fridge.

"I'd love something to drink. I'm not sure what we have so surprise me. Please."

There are some bottles of flavored water. I grab one for each of us and head back. I grab two different flavors, figuring she can just pick whichever she likes best and I'll drink the other. She turns on her side, remote in hand and flipping through the channels. She smiles up at me and tilts her head behind her. The sofa is deep, plenty of room for me to lay with her. I put our drinks on the wooden side table and kick off my shoes before she turns onto her back. I stretch out on top of her, then shift my weight so I'm lying next to her. She follows me, turning to face me.

"Hey," I say pushing her hair off her face and tucking it behind her ear.

"You are really here."

I ham it up, looking around before smiling at her and leaning in to give her a kiss.

"I don't want to go to work tomorrow," she pouts.

I grin.

She smirks at me and half pushes at my chest. "But I have to. Wanna come in with me? You can see where I work and meet everyone."

"Sure. I can help out if you want me to."

Her eyes twinkle. "Free labor?"

I pull her tighter to me, cupping her ass. "I'm good with my hands."

Her lips find mine, her arms wrapping around my neck. Slowly, lazily, I slide my tongue across her lower lip and into her mouth. Our impromptu make out becomes punctuated with droopy eyes and contagious yawns. She drifts first, her face tucked under my chin, my arms securely around her.

The sensation of her slipping away is what wakes me. I blink open my eyes and it takes me a moment to place my surroundings. I watch Sarah's figure retreat into the kitchen, imagining pulling that sundress off of her later tonight. I'm sitting up when she walks back in.

She cocks her head to the side. "I don't really feeling like cooking tonight. How does Chinese sound?"

I grab her hand and pull her into my lap, burying my face in her neck and nipping at it. "You sound better."

"Will." She tries to sound serious, but her giggles ruin it.

"Yes, love?" I breathe against her neck.

She tilts my head up and kisses me sweetly before pulling back. "Sooner we eat, sooner we can go to bed."

And she does not mean for sleep. We end up ordering a couple chicken dishes and a beef one to share. She picks out a movie, and once the food comes, we camp out around the coffee table.

"When'd you learn how to use chopsticks?" I ask, nodding at her hand.

"Sawyer taught me. I can teach you if you'd like."

She goes right into my first lesson, leaning over me from behind, her hand positioning mine. I manage to pick up bigger pieces with the sticks. Rice is not as easy. She laughs at me when I go back to using my fork. After we clean up and put the leftovers in the fridge, Sarah pulls me toward her room.

She walks backward toward her bed, pulling her dress off over her head. My mouth waters just looking at her. I follow her, tugging my shirt off and unbuckling my belt as I approach her. She slips her hands behind her back to unclasp her bra. I step out of my shorts as I watch it fall to the ground. She reaches out to me, pulling me toward her, and we tumble backwards onto her bed. She pushes me down and moves on top of me. My hands lift to stroke and cup her. She leans forward to kiss me. I hold her there, one hand moving to the back of her neck, the other sliding down to hold her hip.

She moves lower, kissing her way down my neck, across my chest, over my stomach. She pulls my boxers down and slips off her panties. I lift my head and watch her take me in her hands. Seeing my cock in her hands only makes me harder. She locks eyes with me as her grip tightens, and she slowly strokes me. When her other hand reaches down to grasp my balls, I can't take it anymore.

I flip her on to her back and cover her. "My turn."

She stretches like a cat beneath me, arching her back until her breasts brush against my chest. I drop my head to taste her lips. She tries in vain to pull my hips down to her. I make my way down her body. I kiss and pull her peak between my teeth, rubbing my tongue over its tip as my hand drops lower to caress her. I love the way her body reacts to my touch, the way her hips buck and her nails bite into my scalp.

"I want you," she moans, rocking against my hand.

I move my hand to her hip and turn her. She helps me, flipping over onto her stomach. I move behind her, lifting her up. She pushes against me, and I thrust into her.

She gasps.

"Did that hurt?" I ask, pausing.

"Don't stop. That feels really good."

God, it feels deep like this, and her ass. Fuck it looks amazing. I grip her hips tightly as I pound her. I think I'm going to lose my mind when she begs me to go harder and faster. I lean over her, holding myself up with one hand and reach around to rub her clit with my other. I'm gone the second she cries out and starts pulsing around me. Holy shit.

We collapse together. I'm scared I'm squishing her, but fuck, I need a second to catch my breath before I even think about moving. She turns her head and finds my lips. I inch off her and pull her into my arms so she's facing me. I don't think she gets how much power she has over me.

She pulls away to set her alarm, and I mourn the absence of her warmth.

"I should be doing something productive," she groans as I fold her back into me.

"Like what?" I ask, kissing her neck.

"Like unpacking, laundry, and I should probably type up a formal memo for the going remote scenarios."

I know she isn't going anywhere when she starts lightly scratching up and down my back. Closing my eyes, I can't even think it feels so good right now. I peek at her when she stops and, my brain starts functioning again. "How about I do laundry tomorrow?"

Her head pulls back as she gives me a yeah right look.

I lean down and kiss her disbelieving lips. "I'm serious. I'm not going to iron them or put them away, but I do know how to wash and dry clothes."

She laughs. "You'd do that for me?"

"It's laundry. I think I can handle it, especially if it means you not leaving this bed anytime soon."

Her eyes widen. "Oh, so that's what this is about."

I nod. "Yes, ma'am. I'm afraid I'm not done with you yet."

17

I groan when her alarm clock goes off the next morning. She turns it off and is in the bathroom starting her shower before I have a chance to even enjoy waking up with her. However, the front row seat to watching her get dressed almost makes up for it.

"Are you going to take a shower?" she asks as she's bent over in front of me just wearing a bra and panties, towel drying her hair.

That just isn't nice. I get up and go shower. When I see what she's wearing, I start to wonder if I need to dress up too. She looks fucking hot. She's wearing this grey skinny skirt that hits her knee but has a slit up the back, a black button up shirt with short sleeves and black heels. Since we didn't unpack, the beige slacks I pull on are kind of wrinkled. My blue polo seems good, though.

I look at her. "Is this okay? I feel like a bum next to you."

She walks over to me, flicking her hair off her shoulder, her hips definitely rocking. Putting her arms around my neck, she pulls my mouth down to hers. I should ask how I look more often. I lean down, gripping her ass and pulling her up on me.

She's breathless when she finally breaks our kiss, and I'm trying to think of a way to get her to call in sick.

"You look good, Will Price, really good."

I lean down to give her another kiss. "You look straight up fuckable. Damn." I shake my head at her.

She grins. "You like?"

I chew on the corner of my lip and nod.

We grab breakfast on the way in. Her office is on the second floor of a simple grey brick building. We're the first ones there. I follow her as she flips on lights. There is a small conference room, a break room, and three offices. The two larger offices each have three desks set up in them. Sarah's office is smaller and at end of the hallway the other rooms are off of. She sits down at her desk and motions for me to pull a chair around so I can see what she does. She barely has her computer up when we hear someone come in.

"How was the—" a woman pauses mid sentence when she sees me. "wedding?"

Sarah stands so I do too. "Cathleen, this is Will. Will, this is Cathleen."

She steps into the office, and we shake hands.

She looks at Sarah. "Today his first day?"

She laughs, putting her hand on my arm. "No, Will is my," she looks at me as she hesitates, "boyfriend." She makes it sound like a question.

I don't want to be her boyfriend. It just doesn't sound serious enough.

Cathleen smiles at me and pops up her shoulders. "It's so nice to meet you. I didn't know you were seeing anyone. I'll get out of your way."

She heads in the direction of the break room and Sarah looks at me. "Was that weird? That felt weird. I didn't even know if I should call you my boyfriend."

I lean down and brush my lips across hers. "I'll be whatever you want me to be."

Her eyes light up as she smiles. "Thanks."

We hear more people walk in, and she glances down at her watch. "That should be everyone. Why don't we head out there, and I can introduce you to everyone else at the same time?"

"Sounds good."

She reaches her hand out to me and I slip her hand into mine. The two offices with the desks in them open up to each other. We stand in the hallway between them, and she clears her throat. "Hey, gang. It's good to be back. I am really proud of the way you guys handled things in my absence. The wedding was amazing. I wanted to introduce you all to Will. We were high school sweethearts and reconnected over the past week. Thought I'd give him a tour and give him a chance to meet you all."

With the exception of Cathleen, who waved at me from her desk, the other employees come over to shake my hand. I can't help but notice a guy named George checking Sarah out. I put my arm around her shoulder and meet his gaze. Uh uh, buddy, all mine. She reaches her arm around my waist and leans into me. She lets them know that after lunch there will be a staff meeting in the conference room before we head back to her office. Once she's up and running, we just hang out while she gets caught up on email.

The silence between us is comfortable. I brought a book with me. Every so often, while she's reading something on her computer she drops her hand down to my leg and just rests it there, like it's the most natural thing in the world to do. I reach down and rest my hand on hers, giving it a little squeeze. I find myself watching her more than reading my book. Her skirt slides up when she crosses one leg over the other. I know she will never go for it with people in the office, but I can't stop picturing how hot she would look bent over her desk. Maybe I can talk her into coming back after hours.

Quarter of twelve, she tilts her head me. "You must be so bored. I don't know why I thought this would be more interesting."

I laugh. "I'd watch paint dry if you were with me."

She elbows me. "Yeah, right."

I smirk. She's probably right.

"So," she continues. "Wanna get out of here?"

"Sure. Did you want to grab some lunch?"

She opens the bottom drawer of her desk to pull out her purse before standing. "Yeah." She glances towards her open office door. "Maybe we can get something to go and eat at my place."

That sounds like code for sex. I grin, message received. We hit a drive thru and book it back to her house. I manage to set the bag of food down on the coffee table before she drags me back to her room. I like a girl who knows what she wants. This is a change from the Sarah I knew back in high school. She was never this bold. I gotta admit change can be good. We make our way back to the living room and eat. Between bites, Sarah asks if I'll be bored while she's at work.

I shake my head. "Don't forget. I got laundry to do."

She softly kicks me. "You really don't have to do that.'

I cock my head at her. "A deal's a deal."

I walk her out to her car and kiss her goodbye. I know she's nervous about meeting with her team so I want to surprise her when she gets home. I start the first load of laundry and hop on the computer. There's a grocery store not far from her place. I grab Sawyer's keys and help myself to her Hummer.

The fridge is on the empty side so I go ahead and shop for her, stopping by the floral section to pick out some lilies. I'm not much of a cook, but I saw a grill on their deck and I can make a mean steak. I pick up all of her favorite things and head back to her house.

I switch the laundry and hop back on the computer. I have my camera with me. Maybe I can find a hiking trail nearby where I can find some good shots. I see a couple promising spots that I can ask Sarah about when she gets home. When I'm done on the computer, I start another load and find a movie to watch. Sarah gets home when I'm starting the third load.

"Hey, you," she says, wrapping her arms around my waist.

I tilt her chin up so I can taste her lips. "How'd the meeting go?" I murmur against them.

She smiles, her lips still on mine. "Good, good." She leans her head back. "Consensus is we let the lease run out and go remote."

The relief is written all over her face. That was the option she was hoping for. "That's great news."

I'm bringing her home. She nods, then holds onto my arm as she leans down to slip off her heels. She squeezes my arm and heads to her bedroom. "I'm going to throw on some shorts."

A couple minutes later, she comes back in with her hair pulled up in a ponytail, small running shorts, and a t-shirt on. Somehow, she looks just as hot as she did in her work clothes. She flops down on the couch.

"How was your afternoon?"

I go and sit next to her, pulling her legs across my lap and tell her about the walking trails and the movie I watched. I'm still waiting for her to notice the bouquet of flowers sitting on the kitchen island. She gets up not long after and goes into the kitchen to open a bottle of wine. She isn't gone but a moment before she races back into the living room and jumps on me.

"Lilies. I love them, and you," she says, peppering my face with kisses.

I grip her hips and deepen the kiss.

She lifts her head, resting it on her hand. "I could get used to this."

I count off on my fingers. "Laundry, grocery shopping, flowers, dinner…"

She cuts me off. "Dinner?"

I nod. "I picked up some steaks."

I forget all about dinner when she licks her lips. She has no idea how sexy she is. I pull her down and capture her lips. We're interrupted when her phone rings. She ignores it at first, letting it go the voicemail but whoever called just hung up and called again.

She sits up, pouting. "I should see who that is."

I grumble as she gets up, even though I enjoy watching her ass as she walks away. Swinging my legs off the couch, I get up to get dinner started. I'm on her deck heating up the grill when she comes out and wraps her arms around my waist. I close the lid and turn around to face her. Sliding my hands up to her face, I kiss her. She leans into me, slipping her fingers through my belt loops.

"Who was on the phone?" I ask against her lips.

She pulls back, rolling her eyes. "A timeshare pitch. Ugh."

I pull her closer, wrapping my arms around her shoulders and tuck my face into her neck. She smells so good, like pears mixed with vanilla. I rub my nose against her earlobe, and she purrs. I'm ready to strip her down right here on this deck and see what other sounds she might make when I touch her. I refrain, though. It's broad daylight, and I don't want to shock any of her neighbors. I turn both our bodies and check the grill.

Sarah takes a step back towards the door. "Want a drink?"

I follow her to the kitchen to grab the potatoes and steaks. I have a beer and she has a glass of wine while the food cooks. She wipes off their patio table, and we eat out there. After dinner, we take a walk around her complex. She wants to show me the pool and weight room that I can use while she's at work. One of her neighbors, a blonde guy around our age, is walking out as we walk back in.

"Hi, Sarah. How was the wedding?" His eyes pause on our linked hands.

"It was great. Thanks. Oh," she smiles up at me. "This is my boyfriend, Will. He's spending the summer with me. Will, this is Paul."

I have to drop her hand to shake his. When I'm done shaking his hand, I drape my arm across her shoulders.

"I didn't know you had a boyfriend." He's not as tall as I am, which gives me the satisfaction of looking down at him. It's weird. Twice now in the same day I've witnessed two different guys giving her the look. I glance down at her. She has no clue, which makes me feel pretty fucking lucky that I'm the guy with his arm around her.

She bumps her hip into mine. "Will and I go way back."

I lean down and kiss the top of her head.

"Well, it was nice to meet you," he says before heading to his car.

We turn and make our way up the stairs to her place. "I think that guy has a thing for you," I tease.

She squints at me. "Paul, no way."

I nod. "I'm a guy. Trust me, he does."

She puts her key in the lock. "Sawyer said that too. I still don't think so."

"It's cool. He can look, but you're all mine."

"Ooooh possessive?" She drops her keys on a table by the door and wiggles her fingers at me.

She squeals when I grab her by the waist and throw her over my shoulder, kicking the door closed behind me.

"Will," she gasps. "What are you doing?"

I carry her to her bedroom. "I'm about to show you how possessive I can be."

She giggles when I toss her on to the bed and crawl over to her. She's wearing tennis shoes with little ankle socks. My mouth is on her calves as I slip them off of her. She's ticklish, and I can't resist running my fingers across the bottoms of her feet. She kicks her feet away from me and tucks them behind her.

"I'm going to get you for that," she taunts, beckoning me to come to her with her finger.

I pull off my shoes and launch myself at her. She's flushed and laughing once I have her pinned under me. It is such a turn on, the way her body reacts to mine. I drop my lips to her neck to feel her pulse racing against them. She tries to pull her arms free, but I shake my head at her.

She huffs then pouts trying to grind her hips against mine. I know what she wants, and I plan to give it to her but first I want to see how worked up I can get her. Her chest is heaving and the way her breasts rise and fall with it is too distracting to ignore. My lips and teeth tease her over her shirt and bra. I want to taste her skin.

I move her hands above her head so I can hold them both in one of mine, freeing the other. She arches her back, pushing her breasts up higher. I reach down to lift her shirt, exposing her bra and pull the cups down freeing them.

"Oh, God," she pants when I tongue circles over her. "I want to touch you."

"I know." I grin and nip her sensitive flesh.

She writhes beneath me, making this whole teasing her thing a lot harder than I thought it would be. I want to devour her and bury myself inside her. I slip my hand into her shorts, my mouth still on her breast, my other hand holding her hands above her head. Her hips move with my hand. Hearing her moan drives me crazy. I kiss my way back up to her lips. I catch her moans with my tongue and consume them. Her eyes flutter open and lock on mine as she breaks. She's the most beautiful thing I have ever seen.

When I let go of her hands, she pounces, tugging at my shirt and helping me pull it off. She pulls off her shirt and slips off her bra before gently tracing my tattoo with her fingertips. She does this, almost reverently. She pulls her hair down and shakes it out. Fuck, that's hot. My hands dive into it as I drag her lips to mine.

Her hands work on the button and zipper of my pants. We're kneeling now, face to face. My lips don't leave hers as we finish undressing each other. As much as I want to, I hold off on plunging into her. I want to touch her and kiss her and extend how fucking perfect this moment feels right now.

I trail my fingertips up her arms and over her shoulders, pulling her closer to me as they drift over her back to cup her ass. God, she has a beautiful ass, plump, full cheeks. I squeeze as I rub my cock against her.

Her arms are wrapped around my neck as she presses her equally ode worthy breasts against my chest. "Will," she breathes against my lips.

"Mmm," is all I can manage.

"Please."

Damn.

I lay her down and settle between her legs. She rocks her hips up to meet me. I pause for one beat to find her eyes. She nods her head, and I fucking bury myself inside her. All rational thought gone, I am lost in her. It's almost sensory overload, and she's right there with me, meeting my every thrust. Her nails bite into my back when she goes first. I was close before, but I'm done for when I feel her tighten and pulse around me.

I sink down to the bed, pulling her into my arms. "I love you," she whispers into my chest.

I tilt her chin up. "I love you too." I brush my lips across hers. We end up spending the rest of the night in bed, her tucked into me, and watching TV until we fall asleep. Her alarm wakes us the next morning. I stay out of her way while she gets ready for work. I head to the kitchen to make coffee. I picked up some muffins and Danishes at the store. I'm not sure if she usually picks up breakfast on the way to work. Thought I could save her time and eat with her if she had stuff here. Her face lights up when she sees her plate.

"You didn't have to do this," she says kissing my cheek.

I pull her into a hug, kissing her neck. "I wanted to."

I turn her and lift her onto one of the stools at the breakfast ~~bar~~. "Coffee?"

She grins. "Please."

I pass her a plate, and she goes straight for a chocolate chip muffin. She's licking a piece of chocolate off her fingertip when I turn back with her coffee.

"Let me get that," I say, sucking her finger into my mouth.

Her mouth drops as I swirl my tongue around her fingertip. "Delicious," I tease, kissing the tip of it.

She stares at her finger a moment, blushing before taking a sip of her coffee. I love that I can still make her blush.

"So what do you have planned for today?"

I lean against the counter. "Swim some laps, finish up our laundry and maybe check out that trail I told you about."

She nods. "Sounds good. Do you want to have lunch together? I can meet you someplace or," she pauses, "come back here."

I grin. "Let's eat here."

When she's done eating, I walk her to her car and give her a kiss to last her until lunch. Paul is walking to his car as I walk back to her place. He's in scrubs. I give him a head nod and watch him slide into a shiny Benz. Is he a doctor? I shake it off and head inside to change into my suit. It's early out so the pool deck is deserted. There aren't lane lines set up. I noticed that yesterday. It's part of the reason I want to swim early, to avoid kids. I lose count of how many laps I've done when I stop to catch my breath. I think I've done a 500, or twenty laps, which is what I normally shoot for.

"You have great form."

I look up the see a red head sunbathing in front of me.

"Thanks."

She sits up on her lounge. "I'm Amanda. Have you just moved in? I'm sure I'd remember seeing you around."

I shrug. "I'm Will. I live in Atlanta. I'm visiting my girlfriend." Hint. "For the summer."

Her face falls when I say girlfriend. She looks around. "Where's your girlfriend?"

I climb out and towel off. "She's at work. I should be going. It was nice meeting you."

"I'll be around if you need anything," she calls out after me.

I shake my head. No, thank you. Might have to forgo swimming this summer if I'll have to avoid her the whole time. I shower when I get back to Sarah's and finish up laundry. She has a couple pasta salad kits in her kitchen. I'm throwing one together when she walks in. She's wearing these grey dress slacks that make her ass look amazing and a white shirt with ruffles on it. I move the pan to another burner and pull her into a kiss.

"Smells great." She coils her arms around my neck.

"I'm not that hungry now that I have you in my arms," I admit.

We fool around until she almost has to go. She wolfs down a plate of pasta before kissing me and heading back to work. I take my time eating, bringing my plate over to the computer to pull up that hiking trail again. When I'm done eating, I head out, my camera and a bottle of water resting on the passenger seat next to me.

Sawyer's Hummer has GPS. I don't plug in the address, but I do pull up the map so I can tell when my turns are coming up. It's warm out, not humid like Atlanta. I find the start of the trail and park. It's a nice day, so I'm not alone. There are bikers, joggers, and families hiking. That's a good thing for me. I like people in my shots.

I walk around until my water bottle is half empty and make my way back to the Hummer. I do a double take when I see the time and book it back to Sarah's. I want to beat her back but groan when I see her car. She's in the kitchen pouring a glass of wine when I walk in.

The second I see her eyes I know something is wrong. Is she upset I wasn't here when she got home? "Everything okay?"

She sucks her lips into her mouth and shakes her head, her eyes brimming. I tug her into my arms. She drops her face into her hands and cries as I stoke her hair. "What happened, babe?"

"Cathleen quit. No notice, no reason, just cleaned out her desk and left."

Oh shit. That was the girl I met yesterday. "I'm so sorry." I lean back so I can see her face. "Is there anything I can do?"

"You're doing it," she says drawing me closer.

I grab her glass, and we walk over to the sofa. She takes a healthy swig, and I set her glass down on one of the side tables before pulling her into my lap. She needs support and a shoulder to cry on. I just feel lucky as hell to be that guy for her. I hate that she's hurting. I want to make it better, but in this situation, all I can do is be there for her. I hug her to my chest, lightly rubbing her back. She sits up once to finish her wine and then melts back into me. We stay like that until she admits to being hungry. She goes and changes out of her work clothes while I run out and grab a pizza from a place I passed driving back.

She isn't in the kitchen or the living room when I walk in. I set the pizza on the island and go off in search of her. She's in the bathtub, looking adorably pitiful. I lean down to give her a kiss and go back to grab the pizza. I set the pizza on the floor near the tub and undress. She inches forward so I can slide in behind her.

I reach down and grab us each a slice, holding hers as she leans back against me. When I saw her tub that first night this was not how I pictured us in it. Before today, I have never taken a bath with someone or eaten in one.

We each have a couple slices before she turns and faces me. Bringing her hands up, she lightly holds my face as she kisses me. "Thanks, Will," she murmurs against my lips.

I wrap my arms around her waist. "Anytime, Miller Lite."

She tucks her face into my neck, and I hold her until the water starts getting cold. I get out first and wrap a towel around my waist, grabbing another to wrap around her. She stands in front of me as I move the towel over her skin. I lead her into her bedroom and pull out one of my old t-shirts for her to pull on. She doesn't argue as I tuck her into bed. I drain the tub and put the leftover pizza in the fridge before joining her.

She curls up into me, and I watch her as she falls asleep. The moment I found out at the wedding she still loved me I knew we were going to be together. I just assumed we'd date for a year before I asked her to marry me to be sure we weren't rushing things. As I lay here watching her sleep, after comforting her tonight, I know I don't want to wait.

When her alarm goes off the next morning, she gets upset again when she realizes Cathleen won't be there today. I wish she didn't have to go, but she needs to be there more than ever now that they're short staffed. I offer to try and help, but she refuses, giving me a kiss. When she leaves, I go swim laps. The red head isn't there, which relaxes me. Sarah isn't able to come home for lunch today. I end up uploading all the pictures from my hike and work on cleaning them up in Photoshop for most of the day.

When Sarah gets home, she looks exhausted. We sprawl out on the couch and eat leftover pizza. When we head to bed, she surprises me when she asks me to make love to her.

"Are you sure? No offense, babe, but you look like you're ready to pass out."

"Please."

We slowly undress and move to the bed. There's no teasing, no foreplay. I slowly ease into her, and we kiss as I gently rock in and out of her. There's no crash, no falling apart, just a subtle build until we both feel it, this intense wave of pleasure flows over us. I turn so we're on our sides, and we fall asleep like that.

While she's getting ready for work, she mentions she has to go to Chicago the end of next week for a conference. She asks if I want to go with her, but I see it as an opportunity to buy her a ring. I tell her I don't want to be in her hair and I'll just hang out here. The bummed look on her face when she tells me that's all right kills me. Once she's out of the house, I call her parents.

With the time difference, I know they're up already. I talk to Mrs. M first. She's not a hard sell. The second I tell her I want to ask Sarah to marry me, she screams and asks how soon we'll start giving her grandbabies. Mr. M is not as enthusiastic but gives me his blessing.

Next, I call Sawyer. She doesn't answer, and I end up leaving her a message. She texts me later on, asking if she can call me the next day. I text her back the time to call me.

Whether it's the weekend to look forward to or the shock of Cathleen quitting had worn off, I'm not sure. We go and see a movie, a loud, escapist action movie. Sarah turns her head into my shoulder a couple of times, and I let her know when it's safe to look again, just like we did in high school. We stop for ice cream after, holding hands across the table as we eat.

The next morning, I use the excuse of running to the store to be out of the house when Sawyer calls. After I ask how things are going with my mom, I get right to the point. "I need your help," I plead.

There's a pause. "What can I do for you, William?"

Typical Sawyer. She sounds like the friggin Godfather. I can almost picture her stroking a fluffy white cat as she rubs her chin.

"I want to propose, and I wanted your opinion on the ring."

No pause. "Yes! I'll help. When? Where? What time? This is going to be so much fun." It all comes out as one giant stream of words, and she isn't done. "Have you asked her dad for his permission? You know she'll eat that shit up, and you're tight with her folks so he'd never say no."

She pauses for maybe a second for me to reply. When I'm not fast enough, she keeps going. "Well? Did you? If you haven't we should hang up right now so you can do it. You can call me right back. I—"

"Sawyer!" I interrupt. "I already did that."

"Oh, sweet! All right, Mr. Price. Where do you want to meet up?"

I switch the phone to my other ear and tell her where to meet me. Sarah has to fly out to Chicago for some industry seminar thing. I'll pick Sawyer up from the airport, and we can head straight to the jewelry store. She can catch a flight out the next morning, and Sarah will never know the difference and my mom will be fine on her own for one night. I glance up at Sarah's condo. I had used the excuse of driving to the store for some milk for our call. I catch her peeking out the blinds from the kitchen.

"Hey, I better go," I say to Sawyer before hanging up. I collect the grocery bags and make my way to the door. Sarah pulls it open just as I start shuffling bags trying to get the right key out.

"Need a hand?" She reaches out to try and lighten my load.

I lean forward and brush my lips across hers. "I got it. Thanks for opening the door."

I walk past her and into the kitchen. She closes the door behind me and follows me. I start unloading stuff onto the center island.

She laughs at my purchases. "Oreos, whip cream, Slim Jim's. Oh wait, something healthy." She says lifting the carton of strawberries. "I thought you were just going for milk."

I pick her up, placing her on the island in front of me and nip at her neck. "It all looked good, but now I'm home, you're the only thing I want to nibble on."

She coils her arms around my neck, inching herself closer to the edge of the island, closer to me. My hands are still on her hips, my grip tightening on them as her mouth finds mine. I can't get enough of her. We've been like this since the day after the wedding, almost like we're making up for the last seven years. She starts tugging at my shirt.

I smile against her mouth. She loves touching me. Hell, I love her touching me. I nip at her bottom lip before pulling away from her to take off my t-shirt. When I'm in her grasp again, her hands roam over me. She starts with her palms flat on my chest, pushing them up to my shoulders then down my arms.

She barely touches me with her fingertips. It gives me chills, and I jerk. She loves it. I lift my head to stare down at the impish look in her eyes. This girl, she owns me, lock, stock, and barrel. She looks up at me and wets her lips. I growl, grabbing her by the back of the neck and bringing her lips to mine. Gone are her gentle fingertip touches. Now her nails bite into the skin on my back as she presses herself against me. My fingers tangle in her hair as my lips move down her neck to her chest. I reach for the hem of her shirt.

I lift my head to pull it off, her nails leaving my back to unclasp her bra. She shrugs it off, and I drop my head to say hello to my favorite breasts on the planet. As I kiss and suckle one, I cup and toy with the other, not wanting it to feel ignored. Sarah puts her hands behind her, arching her back. All I can think is how bad I want to be inside her right now. I lift her, thanking the inventor of yoga pants and their elastic waistbands. I tug her pants and underwear down before setting her back on the counter. She lets out a little squeak as her perfect ass hits the cool granite.

I unbutton my shorts and push them and my boxers down my legs, kicking them somewhere when they reach my ankles. She reaches for me, already lining me up. I can see all how bad she wants me inside her right now all over her face. I don't pause. I fill her. She wraps her legs around me as I slowly rock into and out of her. The way she looks at me, God, I'd do anything for her. She's it for me. By some miracle, she starts pulsing around me, and I'm a goner. I groan into her neck as I erupt. After a moment of just holding her, waiting for my heart rate to go back down, she speaks. "You so need to put the milk in the fridge."

When I give her a look, she reaches around to squeeze my ass. "And you rock my world, stud."

I nod. "That's more like it."

We help each other dress, and it's honestly turning me on again. Part of me wants to drag her to her room and start all over again, but I need to reserve some strength for tonight.

Later that day, we go to the pool together. Sarah gives me a look when Amanda waves and calls out my name. "She seems friendly." She does not say it as a compliment.

"She introduced herself the first morning I swam laps," I explain, kissing her cheek. She's cute when she's annoyed. Besides, she has to know I'm solely interested in her. She reads a book on her eReader while we lay out. Every so often, we get in to cool off. Without giving everyone too much of a show, she straddles me and we kiss. I chuckle to myself when I notice we're pretty close to where Amanda is sitting.

"You're not jealous, are you?" I whisper in her ear.

She rolls her eyes but doesn't argue. "You have no reason to be." I nip her ear.

I catch her smile before she looks away. After all the sun at the pool, we take a nap. We grill for dinner and hang out on the deck until the sunsets. Talking about the pictures I took the other day leads us inside so I can pull them up on the computer. I haven't edited all of them, but I show her the handful that are my favorites. I also pull up the picture of the girl who fell off her bike, the picture I won the award for, so Sarah can see the reason we ended up being on the same flight.

It's an unexpected sensation, how pride reflected in her eyes as she looks at my shots makes me feel. It's the confirmation I never knew I was searching for. After some begging, I get her to agree to let me take some pictures of her tomorrow. When we fall asleep again with her wrapped in my arms, I start to wonder if I'll even be able to sleep alone when she goes to Chicago.

The next day, we drive out to the spot where I hiked. It's early and not as crowded as the last time I was here. Sarah wanted to sleep in, but morning light was the best for the shots I wanted to take. I have her stand in front of the rising sun, facing me, away, left, and right.

She lifts her hands to cover her eyes when she faces away from me, the glow of the sun all around her. That's the one. We hit the grocery store on the way home to buy real food. After that, we hang out, watching movies, her sprawled out on top of me on the sofa. The perfect chill day.

The next morning, when it's time for her to leave for work again, her absence strikes me. It's unrealistic to expect her to be home all the time. I'm used to being on my own or with my mom, which really is the same thing in a way, but it surprises me how empty the place seems when she goes to work.

I swim laps and talk to Brian for a while after lunch. He and Christine had a blast on their honeymoon. He's taking a couple extra days off to recover before he goes back to work. I tell him about Sarah and the whole Cathleen thing. He wonders if it's the remote thing that made her leave or if she was planning to do it all along. Either way, he's happy I'm there for her.

"So when are you proposing?"

I shouldn't be surprised. "Your mom told you?"

"Yep, right after she asked if Christine was pregnant yet."

I laugh, remembering the grandbabies she requested of me. "Sawyer's going to fly out Thursday to help me pick a ring out."

We end up talking about my mom, and Brian promises to drop in on her when Sawyer comes out here before we hang up. On Wednesday, Sarah works from home to prep for her trip. I make it my mission to distract her. It's hard not to. She wears an old pair of jean shorts and a black tank top.

She has her laptop set up on the island and sits with one leg crossed over the other. As she works, her leg sways back and forth. It's hypnotic. I stand next to her, sliding my hand up her thigh, waiting for her to tell me to stop. She doesn't; she just arches her brow at me and opens her legs.

18

Since she's only staying in Chicago overnight, she drives herself to the airport and leaves her car there. I'm set to pick up Sawyer at two in the afternoon. Her flight is delayed so I have to hang out for a bit. When she does come out, she's easy to spot with her pink hair.

"Hey, Sawyer."

She didn't check a bag, so I carry the small rolling suitcase she brought.

I hesitate when we get to her car before handing her the keys. I have a list of jewelry stores we can check that are nearby.

Her eyes drift over the list. "Lame, Will. You are not buying Sarah's ring from a mall."

I smirk at her. "Alright, Cheer Bear. Where are we going?"

She grins. "Cheer Bear. I fucking love it. I approve of said nickname, and don't worry about where we're going. Just buckle up."

After fifteen minutes alone in the car with her, it's clear why she worries about having a car accident. She drives like a tweaked out crack head looking for a score. She changes lanes for no apparent reason and gets so far up the ass of any car in front of her she probably owes them dinner. I'm not proud but I hold onto the door handle the whole ride. She's heading north of where their place is. I try to take my mind off her driving by asking about my mom.

"She's just stuck, Will, you know."

I guess that makes sense so I nod. "Have you had anymore disagreements?"

She shrugs. "Your mom is used to getting her way. We're working on that."

"That sounds cryptic."

She nods. "Don't worry, Will. Your mom and I are getting along great."

She pulls up in front of a simple antique store in a strip mall. She flashes me a grin before hopping out. I follow her, scratching the back of my head.

"Here? Are you sure about this?"

She turns, facing me. "Stop being so judgey. Have a little faith."

My hand slices the air with an after you gesture. Have a little faith? I am so outside my comfort zone right now I don't even know what to do. There are so many different kinds of rings out there. It seems almost impossible to pick the right one without her help.

The shop is not well lit, and there is a distinct musty smell to the place.

"Hey, Petey!" Sawyer calls out. "You here?"

A mumbling sound precedes the short thin man who wanders out from a back room. He adjusts the thin framed glasses on his nose before looking at Sawyer.

"Well, I'll be. Come here and give an old man a kiss."

"Way to sound pervy, Petey." She grins before kissing his cheek.

He notices me. "Bringing a boyfriend for me to meet?"

She follows his gaze to me and laughs. "Nope, 'fraid not. Will here is about to ask my best friend to marry him. Brought him here to look at some rings." She hooks a thumb at the cabinet behind her. "How's about you bring out the good stuff?"

He tilts his head to the side as he appraises me, pretty sure the places at the mall would only care about my credit card. He looks back at Sawyer. "Be a dear and flip the sign."

She bounces back on her heels, rubbing her hands together before reaching behind me to flip the sign on the door from open to closed.

"Get the lock too." He calls out over his shoulder as he heads back to the back room.

After the door is locked, we follow him, waving our way through randomly placed cabinets full of orphaned keepsakes. There is a curtain functioning as the doorway. Sawyer pulls it to the side and slides it into a brass half circle. Petey sits at an old Presidential oval office style desk in a rust shaded swivel chair. His back is to us as he pulls three trays, stacked one on top of another, from a safe. Sawyer motions for me to sit in one of the two mix matched wingback chairs that face the desk.

Petey sets the trays on the desktop, separating them and pushing them closer for us to see. My mouth drops at the rings in front of us. They look like museum quality pieces. My eyes flick up to the amused look on his face. We both know I was not expecting this. Sawyer's grinning next to me.

"What if the ring I pick doesn't fit her?"

He shrugs. "Having a ring sized is not a big deal."

I start to look at the rings. I know Sarah will want something simple, elegant. That eliminates the meteor sized rocks right off the bat. I'm looking at the rings on the third tray when I see it, the perfect ring. I pick it up and hold it toward the light to get a better look. Petey describes it as I look at it.

"That's a beaut, platinum band and setting. It's square cut, one carat, with eight smaller stones set in the band. I have the matching wedding band for that ring as well."

I look at Sawyer. She nods.

I frown and look back at Petey. "Do you know the history of this ring? It seems like something that would be passed down in a family."

He smiles, swinging his chair back to the safe and pulls out a royal blue velvet box. He passes the box to me, and when I open it, I see the matching wedding band. "This ring belonged to a sweet woman named Whitney Stone. She was married to Samuel Stone for sixty five years before they passed. They never had any children. They were animal lovers. When they died, their estate went to the charities they supported in life. I purchased this ring and band at an auction and have had it for the last fifteen years."

I pull the band out of the box, and my jaw drops at its inscription *W & S Forever.*

"I'll take it."

The box feels weird in my pocket. The only thing I've spent more for at one time was the down payment on my condo. I hope she loves the ring. I'm not sure Petey has a return policy. We're halfway back to the house when Sawyer clears her throat a couple of times.

On the third time, she adds. "Anything you'd like to say to me?"

Shit. "Sorry, Sawyer. Thank you. That place was different, but the ring is perfect. I think she'll love it."

She smiles and glances at me out of the corner of her eye. "You're very welcome. Petey's a cool dude. I had a feeling he would have what you were looking for."

"How'd you know that guy anyway?"

She shrugs. "Long story." Then she turns the radio up, effectively ending the conversation.

Once we're back at the condo, she asks if I have plans for dinner.

I must look confused. "Not really. You and Sarah are the only people I know here."

"And Amanda," she snorts.

Great. I guess Sarah told her about her. I smirk. "Want to meet our friend Jared?"

That name sounds familiar. "Sure. But how will we explain my meeting him to Sarah?"

She waves me off. "Tell her I told him to come make friends. You need a friend, Will."

I shrug. "Okay."

She shimmies over to her purse and calls him. They talk for a couple minutes, and she flashes me a wink and thumbs up combo. I pick up my phone and text Sarah that I miss her. She replies almost immediately that she wishes she was sleeping in my arms tonight. Me too, I reply.

When Sawyer hangs up, she comes and sits cross-legged on the ottoman-styled coffee table. "We're going to meet Jared for sushi. You like sushi, right?"

"Sushi's good." I pull the velvet box out of my pocket and open it.

"So how are you going to propose?"

I smile. I'm not sure where or when, but I do know how. "You'll just have to wait and find out from her."

She crosses her arms over her chest. "No fun. I think I should get to know because I helped you find the ring."

I snap the box closed and stand. "I'll think about it."

I walk to Sarah's room and hide the box in the drawer she cleared for me. I turn around to see Sawyer in the doorway. "I'm going to shower and change. Be ready to go in an hour."

She turns and walks away after I nod. I look down at what I'm wearing. Jeans and a dress shirt should be fine for dinner. I lie down on Sarah's bed, pulling her pillow to me and inhaling. I wish she was here. Sure, her being gone helped with the ring purchase, but now that it's safely hidden, it'd be nice if she were flying home today. I hang out while Sawyer gets ready. When she walks out of her room, she looks pretty dressed up for dinner.

"Should I change?" I ask, suddenly feeling undressed.

"Nope. I just felt like dressing up. No reason." Sounds like she's trying to convince herself.

On the white-knuckled, gripping-on-to-the-door-handle ride over, she talks about my mom. She's vague. She tells stuff I already know; my mom is stubborn. She's temperamental, and I enable her. She won't get more specific than that. I figure I'll just wait and talk to Brian tomorrow. While we walk up to the restaurant, Sawyer fidgets with her purse. A guy in jeans and a polo waves as we approach.

He pulls Sawyer into a hug and kisses the top of her head, making her blush. He cocks his head at me but addresses her. "So this is him?"

She nods, bouncing back on her heels, and he reaches out his hand to me. "Nice to meet you, dude."

His grip's solid. I'm tall, but he has at least a couple of inches on me and is built. Sawyer looks tiny next to him. Inside, we're seated in a booth. Sawyer sits next to Jared, and they face me. I don't know Sawyer that well, but there is definitely something going on with them. Whatever it is, they use me as a distraction. I now understand what an inquisition might feel like. None of the questions are out of line. I'm just not used to it. I can tell he's just looking out for Sarah. That makes him all right in my book.

We exchange numbers. He has a flexible work schedule and knows a bunch of cool places I can take some pictures. Having someone to hang out with while Sarah is at work will be cool too. When it's time to leave, Sawyer surprises me by handing me her keys and saying Jared will drop her off later. I make no comment.

Sarah calls right as I'm parking. The conference dinner is over so she's back in her hotel room missing me. I spend the next hour going into detail of just what I would do to her if she was with me right now. It's like high school all over again, neither of us wanting to hang up the phone. I fall asleep with the sound of her breath in my ear.

I wake up with a stiff neck and drool on my phone. At some point overnight, my phone died. I'm surprised its low battery chirps didn't wake me. Maybe her phone died first. I get up and plug it in before hopping in the shower. I'm not sure what time or even if Sawyer came home last night. I'm making coffee when she saunters out of her room. I offer her a cup, but she shakes her head, opting to make herbal tea instead. She doesn't need to be at the airport for a couple hours, so she spends the morning telling me cool places around town where I can propose.

What she doesn't know is I have it all planned out, but I humor her anyway. I want to ask her what her deal with Jared is, but I don't know her well enough and she's Sarah's best friend. I'll let her figure it out. Sawyer lets me drive to the airport. Which is a relief. I drop her off instead of parking but do get out to thank her again for helping me find the perfect ring. She punches my arm and salutes me before heading into the terminal.

Sarah's flight won't be landing for another three hours. I kill time by swimming some laps. I'm relieved when I don't see Amanda, until I see Paul. He waves and walks over as I towel off.

"Did I see Sawyer today?"

I don't know. How many pink-haired girls does he see on a daily basis? "Yeah, but she took off today."

He rubs his jaw. "That girl's a wild one."

And my soon to be fiancée's best friend. "Excuse me?"

"Sarah's out of town, right?"

I'm not sure what his point is. I shoot him a confused look.

He lifts his hands and starts to walk away. "If you're into that kind of thing."

I stop him. "I know you are not implying something happened between Sawyer and me."

He shrugs. "Pretty convenient she comes into town while Sarah's away."

I shake my head. "Not that it's any of your business, because let's be clear it's not. She flew in to help me pick out an engagement ring for Sarah."

His jaw drops. Fucking douche. Once I get back to Sarah's, I start cooking. I want to surprise her so I'm making dinner for her. She sends me a text when she lands, and I watch the clock until I hear her keys in the door. She's barely in the door before I pull her into my arms.

"This is a nice hello," she whispers against my lips.

I check the timer on the oven before sweeping her into my arms. "I'm just getting started."

Later, when the buzzer goes off, it's a struggle to untangle myself from her. I manage, and after pulling on my boxers, jog into the kitchen to turn off the oven and set my chicken dish on the stovetop. The smell brings a robe clad Sarah to investigate.

"Smells good," she says, wrapping her arms around my waist and resting her cheek on my back.

I rest my hands on top of hers. "Your mom gave me the recipe, said it was foolproof. Want to eat on the deck?"

While the food cools, I pull on a shirt and some shorts, and she slips on a strapless sundress.

As she carries a bottle of white wine and some glasses outside, she tells me about her conference. "It's a good source for potential clients. I almost ran out of business cards to give people."

Her face is glowing, but it's not hard to tell she's tired. "Did we stay up too late talking last night?"

She pours us each a glass as I set her plate in front of her. "Maybe. Is it cool if we crash after dinner?"

I nod. "We can sleep in tomorrow too, stay in bed all day."

She sighs. "That sounds perfect.'

She has to hire someone to help her handle all the traveling. This week has gone by, and she's only been home one night. Part of me feels like what's the point of my being here if she isn't. What's worse is I don't even feel like I can say anything about it without making her feel bad about the whole situation.

I have this ring burning a hole in my pocket and no girl to propose to. Only good thing that happens all week is the talk I have with Brian. When he went to check on my mom, she actually talked to him. Which is kind of a big deal. And not just that. She gushed over Sawyer. Seriously, didn't see that coming.

So here I am. Things are going good at home with my mom so I know I should stay here, but here sucks since Sarah is gone all the time. Jared and I have hung out a couple of times, played basketball, gone hiking. He seems cool. I'd just rather be with her.

At least it's Friday. She'll be home for the weekend. Sawyer told me the name of her favorite restaurant in town. If she's not too tired, I want to take her out to dinner tomorrow. Her flight lands late tonight, but I make her promise to wake me up.

When she does, it takes me a minute to figure out she's real and not a dream. She's undressed and straddling me, kissing my neck. Best damn wake up ever.

"Hey, babe." She smiles down at me when my hands slide up her legs to grip her hips.

She squeals when I flip her over and dive into her lips. This right here, these moments with her, make it all worth it. Sure, I go crazy missing her while she's gone, but having her in my arms reminds me of what we're working for. She tugs at my boxers, and with her help, I push them down.

Tonight is all about needing her. It's a reminder for the both of us. We're desperate, frantically pushing deeper, harder. I lose my fucking mind when she bites down on my shoulder. After that, I'm like a man possessed, and she's right there with me. I'm amazed at where all this energy comes from. I was asleep twenty minutes ago. Now I'm feeling invincible. She screams my name, and I'm gone. She pulls me down to her and holds me.

"Damn, I missed you," I breathe against her neck.

The next morning, on our way to a trail, I stop by the grocery store to grab a snack.

"Want a root beer?" I ask as I drape my arm around her shoulders.

She beams. "We should buy a two liter and make floats when we get home."

Damn, that was not part of the plan, but that sounds good. "Sure, and a couple for the road."

She shrugs. I grab a box of granola bars and the sodas, using a ten to pay.

Before we walk out, I stop at the gumball machines. "I have an extra quarter."

She rolls her eyes and spins her ring. "Can't get anything better than this ring."

"Oh, really?" I ask putting my quarter in the slot.

When the plastic bubble case rolls into my hand I switch it with the one that has the engagement ring in it. I hold her hand as we walk back to the car.

"This looks pretty cool." I say holding it up before I drop it down her shirt.

She half glares, half laughs at me as she pulls her arm into her shirt to retrieve it. "William Price, you are the biggest..." Her mouth drops when she opens it.

She goes to look up at me, expecting me to still be standing next to her. Instead I'm on one knee, in front of her.

"Sarah Louise Miller, you are the beginning and the end of me. I don't want to spend one day without you by my side. You're all I've ever wanted. Will you marry me?"

She covers her mouth with one hand as she nods. I take the bubble from her other hand and slip the ring onto her finger. I just asked the love of my life to marry me in the parking lot of a grocery store, and she said yes. I stand up and kiss her, picking her up and holding her to my chest. Her arms rest around my shoulders as she shakes in my arms.

"I love you so much," I say against her lips.

Her voice wavers as she tells me she loves me too. I open my eyes and gaze into hers, lifting my thumb to wipe the tears from one. The hiking trip had a ploy to get her out of the house and an excuse to stop by the grocery store. I drive back to her condo, my hand on her thigh. She sits quietly next to me, holding her left hand in her right, her thumb brushing back and forth across the top of her ring. She's so distracted she doesn't even notice we're back at her place. I park the car and walk around to open her door. She looks up at me confused.

I hold out my hand and help her out. "Let's get you upstairs."

"I thought we were hiking."

I pull her to me, snaking one hand around her waist and the other to the back of her neck, my lips a breath above hers. Her lips part, her hands gliding up my arms to my grip my shoulders.

"Seeing as how you're my fiancée now." I curve the hand on her waist down to cup her ass. "I think we need to get reacquainted."

She nods and lifts her lips to mine. I hold her tightly, deepening our kiss. We kiss and grope our way up the stairs until we're inside her condo. A trail of clothes marks our path to her bedroom. She's naked beneath me. The only things she's wearing are the two rings I've given her. We make love, slowly at first, eyes locked as I move inside her. Things escalate when her nails bite into my skin, and she urges me to go harder, faster. I move my hand between us and rub her until I can feel her start throbbing around me. I'm close before but that pushes me over the edge. My whole body tenses before relaxing with my release.

"Fuck," I pant, looking down at her.

"Come here," she commands, pulling my face toward her eager lips.

I turn her onto her side, my hands in her hair.

"Want to stay in bed all day?" she mumbles against my mouth.

"Mm hmm."

She eventually gets up, only to grab her phone and call her parents, then Sawyer. I sit up and lean back onto her headboard and watch her. She pulls on a robe and sits at the end of the bed, phone in one hand, her other, now ring clad, hand held up in front of her as she describes the ring to her mom.

She looks back at me, smiling, "Yes, I'll tell Will you say hi, and I promise I'll text you a picture of the ring today."

I crawl forward until I can rest my cheek on her thigh. Her hand drops down to my head, and she gently combs her fingers through it. She calls Sawyer next. I'm not sure if she's going to tell Sarah she helped me find the ring or not. They don't talk long before her hand stills in my hair, and she smacks my shoulder.

It wasn't hard, but I ask "What was that for?"

She hangs up with Sawyer and smacks my shoulder again. "You got Sawyer to fly out here while I was in Chicago. You got to see her, and I didn't." She pouts.

I sit up and push her down onto her back, pinning her hands above her head before I slowly open her robe. "You never told me she drives like a maniac."

She laughs and squirms under me as my fingertips ghost over her side.

"We even had dinner with Jared. Nice guy," I continue before dipping my lips to her breast.

She's panting now, rolling her hips as she grinds against me.

"Do you like your ring?" I ask around her nipple.

"I love it. No more talking. I need you."

Her back arches, and her eyes flutter closed when my hand drops between her thighs. She is the sexiest thing I have ever seen, and she's all mine. I stop teasing her and give her what she wants. The way she reacts to my touch, the feel of her wrapped tightly around me, turns me on even more. Knowing that I get to be with her for the rest of our lives? There's no better feeling.

We spend a lazy day half dressed, and we only leave her bed in search of food. We seem incapable of not touching each other, a hand reaching out, a dust of a fingertip. There's an unspoken inherent fear that this is still just a dream. I know each day that we're together that will slowly wear off, but I feel better, for the time being, with her safely in my arms.

"What kind of wedding do you want?"

She looks off to the side and pauses while she thinks. "I don't need anything as big as Brian and Christine's. Something simple and small. What about you?"

I pull her hand to my lips and kiss. "Simple and small sounds perfect. When would you like to do it?"

She shrugs. "Part of me wants to drag you to Vegas and do it tonight."

I laugh, and she leans over to kiss me.

"I can't wait to be your wife, Will."

She climbs into my lap, and I smooth the hair off of her face. "My wife," I repeat, almost reverently.

She nods, cupping my face and pressing her lips to mine. "You'll be my husband."

"I like the sound of that."

"I don't want to wait long, but I think we should have it back home."

I wrap my arms around her waist. "That makes sense. It's where our families are."

She drops her arms and leans forward against me. "I'm not sure I can handle planning a wedding right now."

I slowly drag my fingers up and down her back, "Let's not worry about that right now. I know you've got a lot on your mind."

She melts further into me. The last thing I want to do is stress her out. "You could always ask Sawyer to plan it."

Her head snaps up. "You're a genius."

"And…" I slide my hand up the back of her neck and grab a fistful of her hair, pulling her head back until her eyes are on mine.

Her lips part. "A sexy beast."

"Damn right," I growl, claiming her mouth.

19

Our summer all to ourselves is over. I have to get back to plan the next school year. Even though classes don't start for another two weeks, I have to go back to work now for meetings and preplanning. Sarah comes back with me, but she's staying at her parents' house. To go from waking up with her next to me when she isn't traveling for work to this sucks. We need our own place. We also need to plan the wedding, and she needs to finish transitioning her team to working remotely.

Sawyer is still staying at my house, in Bethany's old room. I know from talking to Brian and Mrs. M that she's having such an effect on my mom. It takes me seeing it in person to actually believe it. The day we fly in, Sawyer picks us up from the airport in my car. As soon as Sarah's done hugging her, I put my hand out for my keys. No way she's driving us back to my house. When I pull up to my house, I almost drive into our next door neighbor's car when I see my mom outside checking the mail. It has been over two years since I've seen her leave the house.

I hardly remember parking or climbing out of the car. "Mom?"

She looks over at me and nods.

Sawyer walks over to me. "Hey, Mrs. Price. Your boy is back. Say something to him."

She looks from Sawyer to me. "William."

"Hi, mom," I cautiously reply.

Sarah comes up behind me and slips her hand into mine. "Hello, Mrs. Price."

"Sarah."

We walk over to her. Sarah stands behind me as I awkwardly hug my mother.

"So did you decide where we're eating tonight?" Sawyer asks her.

"What?" I turn and look at her.

She walks over to my mom and links her arm through hers. "Your mom and I thought it would be thoughtful to take you guys out to celebrate your engagement. Right, Mom?"

Did Sawyer just call her Mom?

"Yes, the Italian place you like." She looks up at us. "If you two would like to go."

I start to say something, but Sarah beats me. "We'd really like that."

Sawyer and my mom go inside while Sarah and I hang back. The second the front door is closed, I rub my hand over my face and look at her.

"Did you see that?" I shake my head. "I know you saw that, but damn. I'm just not sure I believe it."

Sarah pulls me into a hug. I take a moment to relax before we follow them inside. I'm instantly struck by how different my house feels.

"What happened to the carpet?" I ask looking around. "Did you paint?"

Sawyer winks at me. "There was this leak…"

My jaw drops. "What happened?"

She examines her fingernails. "It really was the darnedest thing. The plumber couldn't figure out where all the water came from."

Hardwood instead of the carpet I had known my entire life and a cream colored paint replaced the striped wallpaper I had grown up with. There's even a new sofa.

Sawyer sees me look at it and shrugs. "It got wet."

My mom watches me from the doorway to the kitchen. "Is it okay?"

I nod. "It looks great Mom, really great."

She inhales and looks around. "I think so too."

Before dinner, Sarah and I go over to her house to drop off her bags and hang out with her parents for a bit. Her mom must have seen me pull up because before we're even out of the car, the front door opens and she rushes out to kiss Sarah and see her ring.

After she's had a good look at it, she comes and gives me a hug. "You did good, Will." She says, kissing my cheek.

Mr. M is in the living room watching a baseball game. He ohhs and ahhs over Sarah's ring. "You got yourself a heck of a guy, kiddo."

"I'm the lucky one, sir," I correct.

Her eyes flick to mine. She mouths, *no I am*.

Then it hits me again. She is sleeping here, and I'm going to be at my house. All I want is to be tangled up in her right now. I try to pay attention to the conversation, but I find myself just lost in watching her. She blushes when she notices my attention is only on her. Her power over me is effortless. Seeing her turn red is all it takes to make me want to make her blush all over.

She subtly asks me to help her carry her bags upstairs. Once we're in her room, I tackle her onto her bed. She doesn't seem to mind as she tugs at my shirt and unbuttons my shorts. I take her, fast and hard. My mouth silences her as she bucks against me. She is so fucking hot. I almost lose my mind when she reaches down to stroke her breast, pinching and rolling her nipple between her fingers. I hook her legs over my shoulders and pound her. When I turn my face and bite her calf, she explodes around me and I detonate as well.

She goes to take a shower and changes for dinner. I change quickly once we're back at my house. Sarah and Sawyer ride in the back while my mom sits up front on the way to the restaurant. My mom is quiet but present during dinner. When Sarah shows her the ring, she surprises both of us by leaning over and kissing Sarah on her cheek. I squeeze her leg under the table, and she covers my hand with hers. When she looks over at me, her eyes are wet. My mom's approval has always meant so much to her.

I drop Sawyer and my mom off and take Sarah for ice cream before I take her back home.

She grins when I tell her where we're going. "Waffle cones?"

I tilt my head to the side. "Like there's another option."

Ownership at the ice cream shop changed a few years back, and I don't come here enough to recognize anyone working. We get our cones and go sit outside. Like old times, I'm done with mine before she is. Some things never change. Watching Sarah Miller lick a drip of ice cream off of a waffle cone is just as hot now as it was when we were in high school. I hate that I have to drop her off at her parents' house. I want her with me. I settle for making out with her in my car in front of her parents' house.

After saying she should go inside for the third time, she leaves. I lean back in my seat and watch her until she's safely inside before pulling away. My mom has gone to bed, but Sawyer is still up when I get home.

She's in the kitchen making a smoothie. I drop my keys on the counter. "Alright, what did you do to my mom?"

She holds her finger up and turns on the blender. Once she turns it off and grabs a glass, she smirks at me. "I know. I'm awesome, aren't I?"

I nod. "I can't believe the change, and you think she's liking the counselor?"

She laughs after she takes a sip of her drink. "I think Evelyn is great and is really helping your mom. Your mom goes back and forth between dealing with her and hating her." She pauses to point at me. "Once I'm gone, do not let her con you into switching to someone else."

I hold up my hands. "I won't."

She leans back against the counter. "I think you should talk to your mom about selling this place."

I open my mouth, but she shakes her head at me and keeps talking. "It's too big for just her, and for her, there are ghosts here. You and Sarah are planning on getting your own place, right? Maybe when you move out, she'll consider getting a smaller place. This is just me, but I think a condo or a townhouse where she'd have neighbors closer would make her more social."

I chew on the side of my lip. "Do you think she'd go for it?"

She narrows her eyes at me. "I was more worried about you. Are you cool with her selling the house you grew up in?"

I almost laugh. "Yeah, I'm cool with that. This place never felt like home. I practically grew up at the Millers'."

She pauses and looks behind me with a faraway look in her eyes. When her eyes settle back on mine, she smiles. "You were lucky to have them then."

We talk a little while longer before I head upstairs to crash.

"Are you sure about this?" I pause before opening her door.

She reaches up to pat my cheek. "I'm long overdue."

I chew on the corner of my lip and open it for her, waiting until she's in and buckled before closing the door.

This isn't the first trip for me. At one time, though, I wasn't sure if my mother would ever go. We drive in silence. Sarah offered to come along with, but I felt this first time it should be just my mom and me. It's a clear day, cool but comfortable out of the shade. After I park, I wait for a moment and watch as she looks around.

I wonder if it seems familiar. I know she went a few times with Dad to visit Bethany. She must sense I'm waiting on her. She turns to me and nods. I get out and walk around to open her door. We walk together to their plots. Dad's stone matches hers. I don't know why that was such a big deal to me when he died, but I'm happy for it now.

It shows they belong together. They match, my graveyard family. Mom hesitates before walking up to touch Bethany's headstone. It's a grey stone with a black plaque. Bronze lettering to identify her as a beloved daughter and sister. Her hand rests there as she dips to lay sunflowers in front of it.

Bright and cheery against the grey stone, they seem out of place, a reminder of the fault in the grand design of a child dying before the parents. My father's stone is slightly bigger, but not big enough to represent a man who seemed larger than life to me growing up. He's still a stranger to me, a silhouette coming and going.

She raises her fingertips to her lips to kiss them before resting her hand on his marker. I take a step back out of respect when she starts talking to him. What I can only assume is her whispered goodbye. My back turned to her, I feel like calling Sawyer to thank her again. Part of me feared my going to Denver might break her. Instead, it was the push, with Sawyer's help, that started her on the path that she is now.

"William."

I turn. "Yes, Mom?"

"Come stand with me."

I pause to touch each of their stones before going to stand with my mother. She leans against me, and I wrap my arm around her shoulder. She's fragile, but I can see it in her eyes, in the way she stands. She's healing.

"So no Crate and Barrel?"

She shakes her head. "No way. There are plenty of other places we can register at. Do we even need to register? What if we just have people donate someplace in our name?"

I look over at her, my hand squeezing her leg. I get not wanting to run into Jessica, but Decatur is not a big enough town to avoid her forever. We're bound to run into her and her fiancé at some point. I suppress a laugh. I still can't believe who she's marrying. It's just weird. Kyle Nelson's mom works in the front office of the school where I work.

Her divorce, the reasons or reason that led to it, had been a huge scandal. Mr. Nelson is a local attorney. Jessica retained him to handle some unpaid traffic tickets. They ended up having an affair, and Mr. Nelson left Kyle's mom for her. Kyle doesn't talk to his dad anymore from what I've heard. I can't imagine what it would feel like knowing your dad is sleeping with someone you used to date.

Also, Mr. Nelson is not a good looking guy. I'm sure he looked different when he was younger but last time I saw him in the grocery store, he was not what anyone would call in shape. I wonder if Jessica's motivation in marrying him is anything other than money. Jessica bailed on college after our sophomore year.

I heard she was doing more partying than going to class. Her parents cut her off not long after. I almost felt sorry for her, but sometimes people dig their own holes. Sarah's gut reaction to stuff in general is avoidance. It's something we're working through, but I can't just let her stew or run. She's so different in her business, so confident.

Sarah's quiet as I drive her and Sawyer to the airport. We got the news this morning that our offer wasn't accepted on a house we wanted. I know she wanted to have that done before she flew back to Denver. I did too. I'm sick of living apart from her, especially now that she isn't traveling as much for work anymore. It also means the search begins again. We've seen so many houses they all kind of look the same now.

My hand is on her leg while I drive. She puts her hand on top of mine and squeezes it. "Guess what?"

I glance over at her and smile at the expression on her face. I'll play. "What?"

"Next time you pick me up from the airport, it will be because I live here."

I turn my hand over to lift hers to my lips. "I can't wait."

She's only going to be gone a couple of weeks. She needs to do the final walk through of the office space the lease is up on and pack. Since we don't have a place to move her stuff to, she's using a pod and having it moved and stored by us. She hasn't said it, but I know it's going to be rough for her to leave Sawyer. She's giving up so much to be with me. I'm trying to do whatever I can on my end to make it easier for her.

I have a surprise for her that I think will cheer her up. Since my mom has been doing better, she's making a trip to visit my cousins in Italy. That means Sarah and I are going to have the house all to ourselves when she gets back. I haven't told her yet, and Sawyer is keeping it a secret too. Not living together has sucked. At first, the finding time to sneak away here and there to make love was fun and exciting.

Now I just want to be able to fall asleep and wake up with her in my arms. We've gotten hotel rooms a couple of times, but I want more than just one night here and there. I'm going to keep looking at houses while she's in Denver. It'd be nice to have a place before the wedding. She lets Sawyer plan most of it. It's going to be at a bed and breakfast not far from the lake. We reserved the whole place for the weekend. The ceremony will be in their Plantation Hall. There is a separate lake side cabin where Sarah and I will stay our first night as husband and wife. Brian is going to be my best man and Sawyer the maid of honor.

Sarah's going to wear her mother's wedding dress, and the reception will be at the B&B. We didn't invite that many people, maybe twenty total, including us. We thought about trying to honeymoon over winter break, but the end of year can be busy for her workwise so we're planning on going away over spring break. My biggest decision during the wedding planning process is the deciding vote on the wedding cake flavor. Sawyer and Sarah both like different ones. I'm not stupid. I go with what Sarah wants.

I get to the airport early and park. I just saw an amazing house, and if she's up for it, I want to take Sarah straight over to see it. I wait just past security for her. When I see her, I chuckle to myself. She's pulling her rolling bag and digging through her purse for something. She's also stuck behind a guy trying to walk and read something on his phone at the same time. She looks ready to run him over. By the time she's gotten around him, I've made my way over to her. I skip hellos and grab her face, giving her a kiss that will make her never want to get on a plane and leave me again.

I lift my head to look at her and watch as her eyelids flutter open. "Well, hello there," she purrs.

I take over her rolling bag and drape my arm over her shoulders. "Wanna go see a house?"

She laughs then sees my expression. "Are you serious? Now?"

I nod.

"Have you already seen it?"

I don't want to influence her one way or the other so I keep my voice calm. "I have."

She elbows me. "So what'd you think?"

I turn my head and kiss her temple. "I want to see what you think."

She pouts, which doesn't sound hot but somehow is. I love her lips. Just about anything she does with them is hot. We collect her checked bag and head out to the car. She tries to pump me for information the whole way. I annoy her by pantomiming locking my lips and throwing away the key.

I try to change the subject and ask about Sawyer.

It works. "Something is going on with her and Jared but she won't talk about it, which is not like her."

"Has he already moved in?"

She nods. "He takes over my old bedroom tonight. He moved in last week but crashed on the couch."

I laugh, remembering how he looked at Sawyer when we went out for dinner. "You think he stayed on the couch the whole time?"

She spins her ring. "I don't know. One night, I thought I heard something in the living room, but when I went out and checked, he was alone, asleep on the couch."

She hasn't noticed I've parked yet. I smile and nod at her while she keeps talking about how she knows Sawyer is up to something.

Then she looks around. "Hey, where are we?"

I point to the house across the street and her eyes widen. "It's beautiful, Will." She pauses. "Can we afford it?"

I open my door. "It needs some work."

She gets out and meets me at the front of the car. "How much?"

I shrug. "Come see and find out."

Our realtor is waiting for us inside. It's a two story craftsman-styled house with a foyer and staircase right off the front door. Sarah pulls out a notebook from her purse and starts jotting things down, pro/con style. Pro, love the woodwork. Con, floors are in bad shape. We go through the whole house like that, with Sarah writing in her notebook. Normally, I can read her, but I can't tell this time if she likes it or not.

After our realtor has shown us the whole house, she leaves us in the kitchen to talk about it.

"So what do you think?"

"Hmmmm," she says, noncommittally as she looks at her pro/con list.

"You're killing me. Do you like it?"

She sets her notebook down on the counter and rushes over to me, putting her arms around my neck. "I love it. I want it. I think you do too or there is no way you would have taken me straight here from the airport."

I wrap my arms around her waist. "So you want to make an offer?"

She nods and we call our realtor back in. Since the owners have already moved out, maybe we can close this month, in time to pass out candy for Halloween. The next day, we find out there was another offer on the house, but ours was accepted. Getting the appointment to have the house inspected takes longer than we expect, and we find out the wiring is bad and will need to be replaced.

We negotiate with the sellers and split the difference of rewiring the house with them. It pushes back any hope for closing in October. Then that takes longer than expected, which pushes us past November too.

Now we're sitting here at the closing, Sarah's hand in mine, her other hand with a death grip on the keys. I'm praying this house is worth the frustration. We drive straight there afterward to see it again now that it's ours.

Our footsteps sound too loud, and the walls increase the boom of our voices instead of absorbing them. It's like the first time we saw it together, minus the electrical fire hazard and our realtor. I come up behind her in our new master bathroom, locking eyes with her in the mirror as I push her hair out of the way and kiss her neck.

"Mmmm," she moans pressing back against me.

My hands cup her through her blouse as she grinds against me, her hands reaching behind her to grip my neck. I lower my hands to unbutton her pants, and she shimmies out of them before turning around to undress me. I pick her up and press her up against the wall.

"Will?"

I pause. "Yeah?"

"This is going to be our first time together in this house."

I'm not really sure where she's going with this. "Yeah."

"We should make it memorable."

She wants memorable? That I can do. I set her down and drop to my knees in front of her, pulling one and then her other leg over my shoulders. She's trapped, against the wall. She buries her fingers in my hair as I feast. She probably expected me to stop after I feel her pulsing around my tongue, but she did ask for memorable so I'm just getting started. She has never been quiet, and with the echo of the empty house all around us, I wonder if the neighbors down the street can hear her. Once I've practically sprained my tongue and she isn't speaking English anymore, I lower her onto my cock.

"Was that a good start to memorable?" I whisper in her ear, nipping it.

She looks at me, dazed and nods.

I slowly lift her up then down, matching my thrusts into her. She kisses and nibbles my neck as her nails dig into my back. It doesn't take me long to release. We sit there, wrapped up in each other and catch our breaths.

I kiss her softly before asking. "Memorable enough for you?"

She drops her head, resting it on my shoulder. "I don't think I can walk."

I chuckle. That sounds pretty memorable.

What's worse than having a fiancé and still not living with her? Having a fiancée and a house and not having either. We haven't moved anything into the new place because the floors are being refinished, and we can't have furniture on them until that's done. Buying a house, fixing it up, and planning a wedding at the same time sucks. I feel like I haven't seen Sarah all week. The wedding is Saturday, and the following week is winter break. We're going to spend it moving our stuff in.

I pull up in front of her parents' house. I have to laugh when she takes two steps out the front door then turns around and heads back inside. Some things never change. We're having dinner tonight with Brian and Christine.

She leans over to kiss me once she's in the car, and her lips linger near my neck. "Mmm you smell good. Is that a new cologne?"

She's been pestering me to use the stuff she bought me a couple months ago. I was just waiting until I finished the cologne I already have. I hate to admit this stuff does smell better. I pull her by the neck back to my lips and kiss the sass right out of her. When I lift my head, she blinks her chocolate eyes open and lets out a shuddered breath.

I reach up to tuck a strand of her hair behind her ear. "It was a gift from the most beautiful girl I know."

She wipes the edge of her mouth and smiles. "She's got good taste."

I nod, looking straight ahead as I pull out on to the main road. "She picked me."

We meet them at the same tapas restaurant we went to before Brian and Christine's wedding. The way Sarah acted that night, I never would have imagined we'd be here, six months later, engaged. Christine and Brian are already seated when we walk in.

"Hey, guys," Sarah says, leaning over to kiss Christine's cheek. "Have you guys been waiting long?"

"We just got here," Christine smiles.

Brian looks over at Sarah. "All ready for the big day?"

She looks over at me and holds my hand. "I think so. Sawyer and Jared fly in tomorrow."

When the waiter comes over, we order.

Sarah rubs her hands together when the sangria guy comes over. Watching her take a taste is just as hot now as it was last time. She licks her lips. Christ.

After ordering a glass, she glances over at Christine. "Aren't you going to have some?"

Christine shakes her head and glances over at Brian.

He puts his arm around her shoulders. "We actually have some news we wanted to share with you guys."

Sarah's jaw drops, and she looks at Christine. "Are you?"

"Pregnant? Yes! We're going to have a baby."

Brian drops his arm from her shoulder, picks up her hand and kisses it. I didn't even know they wanted kids right away. Sarah's out of her chair and around the table kissing and hugging them.

Once she's done with Brian, I shake his hand. "You're gonna be a dad."

He laughs and scratches the back of his head. "Crazy, huh?"

I shake my head. "Come on. You guys will make awesome parents."

He glances over at Christine, his eyes warming as he looks at her. "I hope so, man. We are going to start looking for a bigger place. Who knows? Maybe we'll be neighbors."

I lean over the table to hug Christine before we all sit back down.

"There was another reason we wanted to get together with you guys," Christine starts.

"We wanted to know if you'll be the baby's godparents," Brian finishes for her.

Sarah looks at me, and I don't even think about it. I nod. She looks back at them. "We'd love to."

Our food comes out not long after. Sarah excuses herself to go to the ladies' room, and I follow her after a minute for old time's sake. I lean up against the wall outside the door and wait for her.

When she comes out, she laughs when she sees me and leans back against the doorframe. "There a long line for the men's room?" She jokes, crossing her arms over her chest.

I reach out, snaking my arms around her waist and pull her to me.

She looks up at me with those chocolate eyes that own me. "Will, do you want to have kids?"

I shrug, trailing my hands up and down her back. "Do you?"

She smacks my shoulder. "That's not fair. You'll just change your answer to whatever I say now."

I lean down to kiss her. "I want whatever you want," I murmur against her lips.

She does that thing, where she melts into me, like her soul recognizing it was made for mine.

Only Sarah can argue mid-kiss. "You'll have kids, even if you don't want them, because I do?"

I move my lips to her neck. "Yes, ma'am. All I want to do is make you happy."

Her hands move up to either side of my face, turning it so our eyes meet. "That's all I want to do for you."

I shake my head. "You've already done it. I'm just trying to catch up."

She gives me a look that I'm guessing means 'what am I going to do with you?'

We walk hand in hand back to the table. Brian and Christine are leaned into each other, his hand on her stomach. I've never really thought of having a kid, outside of knowing I'm not ready for one right now. Looking at Sarah, her hand warm in mine, I know that if there was anyone on the planet I would consider creating a life with it would be her. I can almost picture a little girl with brown hair and eyes who would own me just like her mother.

I shake off my daydream when Sarah asks what I'm thinking about.

I pull out her chair, whispering in her ear as I shift it forward. "You would be a beautiful mother."

20

The week has flown by, full of last minute disasters and not enough time together with Sarah. Part of me wants to skip the ceremony and the reception just so I can be alone with her. She centers me. I don't feel like myself if I can't see my reflection in her eyes.

"Ready?" Brian pops his head in the doorway.

I look in the mirror and straighten my bowtie. "Yep. You got the rings?"

He winks and pats his breast pocket.

It's a bit of a drive out there. Sarah, Sawyer, and Christine spent the night out there last night. Just thinking of her waiting there for me makes me drive a little faster than I probably should.

Brian glances over at the speedometer. "You know, I can represent you in traffic court, lead foot."

I ease my foot off the gas and gnaw on the side of my lip.

He laughs at my expression. "She's not going anywhere. Trust me."

The inn is a restored old plantation, white, with a wraparound porch on each of its two stories. It's decorated for Christmas, garland and lights are wound around the railings. The lights aren't on yet. It's still light out, but I can already picture how beautiful it will be when Sarah and I head to our own private cabin by the lake. Sawyer and Jared greet us at the door. Guests will be arriving in the next thirty minutes.

"How is she?" I ask Sawyer.

She crooks her finger at me so I lean down closer to her, and she kisses my cheek. "Happier than I've ever seen her."

"Thanks."

She lifts up her fist for a pound dog. When our fists bump, she says, "Potato." Then splays her fingers and adds, "French fries."

I shake my head at her as she walks away. Then I glance over at Jared. His eyes are glued to her as she leaves the room. He looks over at me and shrugs before looking down at his feet. While the guests arrive, Brian and Jared seat them. I'm stuck waiting in a glorified coat closet of a room off to the side. It gives me plenty of time to stress over my vows. I've never been much of a public speaker. Sure there aren't that many guests to see me if I mess up, but I want it to be perfect for her. The pastor signals me when it's time to seat my mom.

"I'm proud of you," she murmurs as we make our way to her seat.

"Thanks, Mom." I kiss her temple.

"I wish your father was here." She gently pats my hand.

I gulp. "I do too, Mom."

Right behind us, Brian is escorting Mrs. M. The pastor, Brian, Jared, and I line up, and the pianist changes from playing nondescript background music to Pachelbel's Canon in D.

Christine walks out first. She carries a cluster of white flowers and green leaves with stems of bubbled glass woven throughout that look like icicles.

Christine and Sawyer are both dressed in knee length black dresses with capped sleeves. I see Brian stand straighter as she comes closer, her eyes on him. Sawyer comes next, smiling and almost bouncing up the aisle, which doesn't seem possible in the shoes she's wearing.

When the music changes, I hold my breath. There's a pause before I see her turn the corner with her dad to make their way down the aisle. My chest swells at that fact. She's all I've ever wanted, and today she's going to become my wife.

She's wearing a veil so I can't really see her face. The flowers she carries are like the others, only with pink flowers as well. She's wearing her mother's dress. It's long with a lace overlay, train, and cap sleeves like the bridesmaids' dresses. I glance over at Mrs. M, who has her arm linked through Chip's and is dabbing her eyes with a tissue.

Sarah and her father stop right in front of the pastor.

"Who gives this woman to be married?"

Mr. Miller clears his throat. "Her mother and I do."

He lifts her veil and kisses her on the cheek before putting her hand in mine. I squeeze her hand, and she mouths hi to me. In my opinion, there isn't a more beautiful woman on earth. She is radiant. I can't stop looking at her.

When we get to the vows, we face each other and I hold her hands in mine. I rub my thumbs across the backs of her hands when I feel them tremble.

I take a deep breath and stare into her eyes. "Sarah Miller. I have loved you for so long I don't know what it feels like to not be in love with you. I also know there are no obstacles that will stop me from loving you, not time, not distance. I will always love you and do everything in my power to make you happy. I vow, until my dying day, to shelter you, protect you, and to love you every day."

My voice shakes during the last part, and I watch her eyes glisten.

She takes a shaky breath and clutches my hands as she begins. "William Price, my Will, my heart, my soul mate. You are the most wonderful man I know. I am honored to spend the rest of my life with you. I vow to lift you up, to meet you halfway, and to love you every day for the rest of my life."

My hand shakes a little as I slip the ring onto her finger. "With this ring, I thee wed."

I feel the band slip over my knuckle as she whispers to me. "With this ring, I thee wed."

"You may now kiss the bride."

I smile, putting my hands on either side of her face as I feel her hands rest on my waist. I dip my lips to hers, my wife.

Our friends clap and cheer around us, but I'm lost in her. After a moment, our kiss breaks and we just look at each other.

I drop my hands from her face and reach for her hand. "Hello, wife."

"Hello, husband," she returns in a husky voice that makes me groan.

We walk out together, her arm slipped through mine, and we're directed with the rest of the wedding party to a room for the photographer. She laughs while I ignore everyone else and kiss her.

"Hush, wife." I silence her with my kiss. Once the room where the ceremony was held is clear, we head back in for pictures. I've never been crazy about having my picture taken. I'd rather be behind the camera than in front. Right now, I don't care. I'm in a daze. I'm married. Sarah is my wife. This wedding seemed to take forever to get here, and now the ceremony is over. I'm too preoccupied to care. Besides I have my slim Canon in my pocket to take pictures with once the professional is done with us.

The rest of the wedding party heads into the reception room while we hang back for pictures of just the two of us.

"How are you feeling, wife?" I breathe into her ear as she stands in front of me, my arms circling her waist.

"Thoroughly wedded, husband." She shifts her ass against my crotch.

"But not bedded, and you better stop what you're doing if you want to go to our reception."

"Or what?" she teases.

"Or I'm throwing you over my shoulder and the honeymoon is starting early."

She turns to look at me. "Promise?"

My mouth drops. "Sawyer and our moms would kill us, but say the word and I'm in."

"Ugh," she grumbles. "We have to at least make an appearance."

"We probably should," I agree.

She holds up her hand to look at her ring. "I love it Will."

"You haven't even seen the best part." I take her hand in mine and slip her wedding band off to show her the inscription.

"When did you have it engraved?" She asks, her finger tracing over the letters.

"I didn't." Her eyes widen as I tell her the story.

"It's like they were meant for us."

"Just like you were meant for me Miller Lite." I lean down to give her a kiss and slip her ring onto her finger a second time.

Once our pictures are done, we give our guests more than just an appearance. We are surrounded by all of our favorite people. There's an open bar, and I've just married the love of my life. We celebrate that. Sarah also stalks Sawyer and Jared, which is fun to watch. I don't know either of them well enough to have an opinion on their body language. That doesn't bother Sarah. She asks me anyways until I shut her up with a kiss.

She complies for a while before pulling back. "Do we know if they booked separate rooms?" Her eyes widen. "Oh my God, Will. What if they're sharing a room?"

"You're a nut. You know that, right? I love you, but you're crazy. What does it matter if they share a room? They live together."

Her brows furrow. "You make a good point."

I kiss her nose. "That, wife, is your first lesson."

She snorts. "Dork. Come on, husband. Your wife wants to dance."

That I can do. Once her parents and my mom call it a night and head up to their rooms, we get an inappropriately decorated golf cart lift to the cabin. It must have taken Brian forever to blow up all those condoms. The cabin is also decorated, rose petals in lieu of birth control.

"Mr. Price?" Sarah leans against the doorway to the master bedroom.

"Yes, Mrs. Price?"

She tilts her head and runs her tongue over her bottom lip. "I could use a little help getting out of my dress."

Bam. Hard.

I hurry over to help her undress, dusting kisses across her skin as each opened button reveals her to me. When her dress pools around her feet, she steps out of it and turns around. I think I'm having a stroke, bare minimum a mild heart attack. I have no desire to seek medical attention. If I die right now, it'll be with a smile. She's wearing this white corset that serves her breasts on a fucking platter and a practically irrelevant thong.

"Husband?"

"Yes, wife," I croak.

"Can you please hang my dress up?"

I have never hung up an article of women's clothing faster in my life. I stand, breathing like I just sprinted a mile, and wait for her to make a move. If she wants me to make love to her, I need a sign because, otherwise, I'm ready to fuck the shit out of her. She steps out of her heels and crawls onto the bed. Her back is to me.

She straightens up, still on her knees, and pulls out whatever magical piece held her hair up so brown waves tumble over her shoulders. Her back is still to me as she fluffs her hair before reaching down and sliding that thong down her legs until it rests at the bend of her knees. She slowly bends over, resting her hands on the bed, and looks back at me.

"What are you waiting for, Mr. Price?"

Buttons fly as I pull my shirt and pants off. I'm apparently not fast enough. She holds herself up with one arm and reaches her other between her legs.

"I'm so wet, Will."

My socks are still on, and my boxers dangle from my right foot as I plunge into her. Her breasts tumble free from the top of her corset. I grip one of them as I pound her. She meets me thrust for thrust. I make a silent prayer to the orgasm gods that she cums soon 'cause I'm not going to last much longer. She goes a split second before I do and drops until she's flat on the bed, causing me to fall on her.

I roll to the side so I'm not crushing her as we catch our breaths.

She looks up at me as I brush a piece of hair off of her face. "I've never slept with a married woman before."

She covers her mouth in mock shock. "How was it?"

I pull her to me and start unfastening the hooks of her corset. "Never having it any other way again."

"Is that the last box?" she asks, wiping her brow. It's an unseasonably warm December.

I grin over the top of the box. "Yep. Where's it go?"

"Kitchen." She follows me and leans against my back once I've set the box down.

I turn so I'm facing her, molding my lips to hers. I pull back a hair. "I hope you like this place because we are never moving again."

She wraps her arms around my neck and leans up to close the distance between us.

"Is that a yes?" I mumble against her lips.

"Mm hmm."

"Get a room," Brian mutters from the dining room, and Christine smacks his arm.

"I was going to wait until we had the house to ourselves to start christening rooms, but if you insist." I sweep her up into my arms and start walking towards the stairs.

"Will, put me down." She laughs.

"But Brian said," I pout as Brian yells, "That's not what I meant."

I set her down, her feet on the first step. She leans into me, chest to chest, my hands on her hips. Cupping my face in her hands, she kisses me sweetly. "What am I going to do with you?"

Her chocolate eyes hold my gaze. "You have forever to figure it out, Mrs. Price."

"We're going to take off." Brian helps Christine off of the sofa, absentmindedly stroking her belly.

She's just barely showing. They come over to hug both of us before leaving.

She turns to me and raises a brow. "Does this mean we have the house all to ourselves and we have furniture?"

I chew on the corner of my mouth before tossing her over my shoulder and carrying her upstairs. Her mouth drops open when she sees our bedroom. "Who made the bed?"

I dip my head to kiss her neck. "Christine."

"Best sister-in-law ever!" She giggles, pushing me onto my back.

The End

ACKNOWLEDGMENTS

First and foremost to my readers, thank you for taking the time to read something I wrote.

Seth, living with me is not easy and you manage to make it look good. I love you baby. To Zach, Aydan and Emma, you three inspire me more than you'll ever know.

My Betas, Amy, Jennifer, Michele, Bobbie, Jenny, Kristy, Anna, Judy, and Vanessa (aka eagle eye). You guys mean so much to me and everyday make me a better writer.

To my formatter, Jovana Shirley, thank you so much for making my book beautiful.

To my editor, Yesenia Vargas, I do not trust anyone else with my words. Thank you so much for cleaning them up without ever trying to change what I wanted to say.

Sarah Hansen with Okay Creations, you have done it again. Your talent and eye make you an inspiration to work with, you also say funny shit that makes me laugh.

There are many authors I now speak to on a daily basis that this book could not have happened without. Kendall, Jennifer, Chelsea, Nicola, Gareth, Karen, and Rachel.

One in particular is Melissa Collins. You are my book wifey and I cannot thank you enough for lifting me up every time we talk.

To all of the blogs that take the time not only to read our books, but also to tell other readers about them. I'd especially like to thank Debra with the Book Enthusiast for another amazing tour. Also, Bobbie and Hetty with Best Sellers and Stellars, Jeannette and Kris and Nicole with I Heart Books, Mindy with Talkbooks, Louise with Hooked on Books, Danielle with Just Booked, Britney with Living Fictitiously, Emily with Rate my Romance, Lisa with Three Chicks and Their Books and any other blog or page that supported me along the way.

ABOUT THE AUTHOR

Carey Heywood was born and raised in Alexandria, Virginia. At eighteen she joined the Air Force to see the world, instead she saw Texas, Maryland and Arizona. Ever the mild mannered citizen Carey spends her days now working in the world of finance, retreating into the lives of her fictional characters at night.

Supporting her all the way are her husband, three sometimes adorable children, and 9 lb attack Yorkie. Inspired by people everywhere her characters sometimes spend chapters learning life lessons while dealing with all the pitfalls that come with falling in love. A self published New York Times and USA Today bestselling author with four books out and many more to come.

In her free time Carey enjoys curling up with a good book. If her family insists she leave the house she has also been known to ski, kayak, and attract Mosquitos. She can make a mean Belgian waffle and has an unhealthy obsession with Swedish fish.

I'd love to hear from you!

www.carey.heywood@blogspot.com
@Careylolo
www.facebook.com/CareyHeywoodAuthor

Coming February 2014

Better

By Carey Heywood

Aubrey is embarking on a bucket list trip around the world, the last wish of her Aunt Ally. It was supposed to be the trip Ally would take when she got better. Now it's just a chance for Aubrey to say goodbye.

Adam escapes in his solo trips overseas, working just enough to fund the next one. When the opportunity to circle the globe falls in his lap he can't refuse. The only catch, he won't be traveling alone this time.

Unable to hide from each other Adam's overprotective nature thwarts Aubrey's desire to find her own way. Can they move past initial assumptions to find something better?

BOOK THREE IN *THE LOVE* SERIES

Let Love Heal

> I laughed and cried as I fell in love with Melanie and Bryan's perfectly imperfect romance.
> - New York Times and USA Today Bestselling Author Carey Heywood

MELISSA COLLINS

Available Now

Let Love Heal

By Melissa Collins

Perfection. We all strive for it, but what happens when the desire to be perfect consumes you? What happens when the need to bury your mistakes blinds you?

Melanie Crane has always been the perfect daughter, friend, student – she's been perfect at everything, in fact. But when she lets her insecurities, the ones that she keeps hidden from everyone, get the best of her, she falters in her pursuit of perfection. Melanie crumples under the pressure and buries her pain. Numbed by sadness and guilt, she is determined never to let anyone find out how broken she really is.

Bryan Mahoney may appear to have everything in order. He's charming, witty and completely swoon-worthy. In short, Bryan has life all figured out, but appearances can be deceiving. When the landscape of Bryan's family changes in an instant, he's left to pick up the pieces.

Not all bruises leave a mark. Now, weary and afraid, Melanie and Bryan must find a way to let love heal their broken and jaded hearts.

A MESSAGE OF Flowers

RACHEL WALTER

Coming Soon

A Message of Flowers

By Rachel Walter

White Carnations - Pure love, sweet and lovely.
Daisy - Innocence, beauty, simplicity.

To florist, Georgina Nickols, every flower has a meaning and a purpose. Flowers are something she knows, lives, and breathes. But when they start mysteriously showing up on her porch, she's unsure of their meaning, and of who is leaving them.

What do these flowers mean to the messenger?

An old friend from high school, Corbin Waylay, moves back to town. When he shows up, he stirs up all kinds of trouble for Georgina. Her life-long friend, Sid Trail, hates him and makes that fact clear to Georgina. But despite the warnings from her friend, she just can't help the feelings that resurface. The feelings she hasn't felt for anyone since high school graduation, the feelings that only Corbin can induce.

As Corbin moves closer into her life, it causes a rift between her and Sid. The mystery flowers continue to appear and begin to add to the stresses of life.

Love, secrets, pain, and lies surround Georgina, putting her trust to the test.

When the messenger is finally revealed, will the meaning of the flowers be enough to repair the damage of those hidden secrets?

Forget Me Nots - Remember me forever, good memories, hope.
Single Red Rose - I love you.

Made in the USA
Charleston, SC
09 January 2014